'Well, it's late. I

'Yes, I suppose…' Sa

Desire stretched between them like a taut, heavy rope. If either tugged, the other would topple and this farce, this forced politeness, would be over. All she had to do was smile, open the door, let him leave, take two aspirin and retreat to her bed, alone, for twelve more years.

But she couldn't leave it like this.

'Alex, aren't you going to kiss me goodnight?'

He took one step towards her. 'I wouldn't dare kiss you, Sarah.' He hesitated for an instant. 'First date, you know.'

'But, Alex…'

His honest admission made the ache in her body more immediate, more demanding than the ache in her heart. She wanted him so desperately, she could barely remember the hurt, the anger, the vows of revenge.

She held out her hand to pull him back into the room. 'It's not our first date now, is it?'

Dear Reader,

Remember that special high school boyfriend? Some of you lucky ladies married him and are still living happily ever after. Some of us lost him to a prettier girl, or said a bittersweet goodbye as we went off in different directions, vowing to be true but quickly finding other boys—men now—and feeling that old flame die.

Then there's Sarah Nevins, beautiful and feisty, whose memories are still feeding the blaze of that first love many years later. He was the one who ended their youthful romantic idyll, and now, out of the blue, he's back, wanting a second chance.

What's a girl to do? Especially when he plies her with flowers and…air conditioners. It's a sizzling summer in New York, and when Sarah and Alex are together, the temperature only rises. The old passion is still there, unabated. All Sarah has to do is forgive him for the past, but can she let go of her need for revenge?

I recommend that you find a cool spot and pour yourself a glass of iced tea before you turn another page of this book. Otherwise, you might find it…*Too Hot To Handle*. Here's wishing you a great summer with lots of time for reading!

Barbara Daly

TOO HOT TO HANDLE

by

Barbara Daly

MILLS & BOON®

This book is for my park friends, those intrepid New Yorkers who walk
their dogs in Washington Square at seven in the morning, no matter what's
going on in the rest of the world or falling out of the clouds above them:
Wanda, Gideon and Crissy; Natt and Nickie; Mary Lou and Emily; Mary,
Teddy and Jordan; Lynn, Boris and Jenny; Marvin, Ziggy and Miss
Daphne; Ann, Pat, Phoebe and Siren; David, Russ and Sally; Marsha and
her Emily; Rozanna and the memory of Tara; Susan, first with Jazz and
now with Ralph; Holden, Calpurnia, Nina, Lucy, Tiger, the sweet Sheltie,
and all their moms and dads; Sandra and Lou, who are actually walking;
and Cecily, my excuse for being there; and New York itself, whose special
qualities make friendships like ours possible. Bless you, and stay strong.

*First published in Great Britain 2003
by Harlequin Mills & Boon Limited,
Eton House, 18-24 Paradise Road, Richmond, Surrey TW9 1SR*

© Barbara Daly 2002

ISBN 0 263 83550 2

21-0403

*Printed and bound in Spain
by Litografía Rosés S.A., Barcelona*

1

"YOU NEED TO GET LAID."

Dumbfounded, Sarah Nevins stared across her desk at Macon Trent, congenital nerd and, as the guy who kept the computers up and running at Great Graphics! her most essential employee. Otherwise, she'd fire him on the spot.

"Don't hold back, Macon," she said, forcing her lips into a tight little smile. "Just be blunt."

"As blunt as you were with Ray just now?"

Sarah's steady gaze wavered. "What exactly did I say to Ray?"

"You told him his copy for the RemCom brochure sucked blood from chickens. It was not your usual management style."

Sarah sank her face into her hands. "Where is he? I have to apologize."

"He's in the rest room crying."

"Okay, as soon as he comes out." She rocked her head from side to side. "I don't know what made me do it."

"You aren't like the Sarah we keep working for in spite of our miserable paychecks. How long has it been since you went out with a man?"

Sarah raised her head to glare at him. "Macon, that's even worse than asking a woman how much she weighs." He needed contact lenses, a personal shopper and a lengthy session with Miss Manners.

"Oh. Thanks for the tip." His reflective pause was brief. "I think your last date was about a year and a half ago. With our cardstock salesman." He lifted an eyebrow. "Our former cardstock salesman."

She gritted her teeth. Even Miss Manners would find Macon a challenge. "I didn't like his yellows. He took it personally."

His other eyebrow winged upward. She gave up the fight. After a deep, mood-changing sigh, she said, "Maybe you're right. Maybe I should start looking around for a new relationship." She, at least, had some manners, some delicacy of expression. But she wouldn't be looking for a relationship, she'd be looking for a man, somebody to satisfy the needs only a man could satisfy.

"Don't do anything foolish."

"Do I ever?"

"Not at the office."

"Not anywhere. I'll meet a man through friends, or find a bonded carpenter or plumber. A union man with credentials."

The search and capture wouldn't be too difficult. Her standards were reasonable and easily met. He should be clean—drug-free, disease-free and addicted to daily showers, deodorants and promising toothpastes—and lacking a record of abusive behavior. Other than that, almost anyone would do. She wasn't looking for a man to share her dreams, make her rich, raise her consciousness, enhance her knowledge or give her a home and children. Many years ago when she was young and hopeful, she'd wanted those things with Alex—Alexander Asquith-Emerson—and she still felt that if she couldn't have them with him, she didn't want them.

"Sarah..." Macon seemed to gather up something within himself as he leaned forward. "These days the world is a dangerous place for women. Maybe I could fill the current void. You and I know and understand each other, and all I feel for you is the deepest respect. No strings. No promises except my promise of total discretion. I could get you over your rough spot."

Today was apparently going to be studded with shocks, so she might as well get used to them. Sarah gazed into his eyes, seeing nothing there but an earnest need to help her out, and as magnified as Macon's eyes were behind the Coke-bottle lenses of his glasses, you could pretty much see whatever was there. But he'd given her an opening to say something to him she'd been wanting to say for a long time, if she could get her mind off her own problems long enough to grasp the opportunity.

"Macon," she said with great solemnity, "I am deeply flattered by your offer, and I'm tempted to accept it. You have no idea how attractive a man you are."

He actually could be, if it weren't for those glasses, his depressing sartorial choices and a haircut that looked as if he'd done it himself. She rarely noticed Macon's looks. She was too dependent on his genius.

"That's what my landlady tells me," Macon admitted. "She's always after me to buy clothes, get a better barber."

Any barber. "Listen to her," Sarah said. "A few outside changes would give you self-confidence. Personally, I'm extremely fond of you just as you are. But I have made a vow not to have sex with my professional colleagues. You saw what happened with the cardstock salesman. When I rejected his yellows, I lost his reds, the best reds on the market." She sighed, still stung by the loss. "Most people have a religion to guide them," she added for good measure. "That's mine."

Macon nodded, apparently not at all hurt by her refusal. "It's one of the things I respect you for. Just thought I'd make the offer. Save you time and hassle."

"I really appreciate it, but you deserve something more."

"Oh, come on, Sarah."

"I'm serious about this. And what I want you to do—" She got up, came around the desk and sat on the arm of his chair. "What I want you to do," she repeated softly, "is go out and find someone who will love you romantically as much as I love you as a friend and colleague. Somebody who will appreciate all those qualities that make me love you. Maybe even—" she put her hand under his chin and tilted his head up until his eyes goggled directly into hers "—maybe even somebody who wants strings, something permanent."

She had him mesmerized. His lips parted. "Why are you so sure you don't want something permanent yourself?"

She let go of his chin and stood up. He'd surprised her again. She felt uneasy, fidgety. "Maybe I just can't see past you," she said in a sexy growl he couldn't possibly take seriously.

In fact, he laughed. "Okay, okay," he said. "Just..." He was grave again. "Just be careful, okay?"

"Absolutely." But not in the way he imagined. She had no fear for her physical safety. All she had to protect was her heart.

THE NEXT MORNING was no different from the last month of mornings. Sarah woke up hot and restless, exhausted from fighting her way through dreams that swirled her into a spiral of desire, then left her floating in limbo, just short of reaching the pinnacle of release. The sheets were damp and tangled. Her nightgown, nothing more than a cream silk slip, felt clammy as she shrugged the slender straps off her shoulders and let it fall to the bathroom floor.

In the shower, she moved the faucet from hot to warm to cool. As she ran nervous fingers through her damp hair, feeling the curls spring up with a life of their own, she felt fresher, but not better. The heavy, swollen sensation persisted, making her feel dull and lethargic.

Coffee should help.

It didn't.

Clothes. Sarah reached into the sea of black that filled most of her closet and drew out a pair of slim capri pants, a tiny, tight tank top and a jacket that looked as though someone had shrunk it, as it was short in the sleeves and short in length.

She frowned at her reflection in the mirror, her mood darkening. What she needed was a splash of bright color. She exchanged the black pants for an identical pair of khaki-colored capris and took a second look at herself. Yes. Very jolly. Practically festive for downtown Manhattan.

She put large gold hoops in her ears and her entire collection of gold bangles on her right arm. They clanked dully in rhythm with her black mules as she traveled the crumbling, tip-tilted New York sidewalks—half of the long crosstown block to Sixth Avenue, then a dozen short blocks uptown—to her office in Chelsea. While she walked, she faced up to her problem.

Those bothersome dreams hadn't been wild and crazy fantasies. They'd been wild and crazy memories, memories of Alex.

Macon was all too right. It was once again time to find a man to dull those memories.

Just a man, that was all she needed. She'd start looking for prospects this very weekend. She only hoped her staff wouldn't move on to greener salaries before she found one.

ALEX EMERSON STROLLED aimlessly north through Soho after lunch in Tribeca, crossed Houston and made his way up to Washington Square. Encouraged by the warmth of mid-May, joggers trotted around the perimeter of the park and dog owners ignored the No Dogs Allowed signs to toss Frisbees to ecstatic black Labs and golden retrievers. In the center of the park near the fountain, hot-dog vendors were doing a land-office business.

The hot dogs smelled great, but he'd already eaten a couple of times today and would have to eat a couple of times more. He had several hours between the long but productive business lunch at Arqua, which he'd just left, and drinks at the Plaza's Oak Bar with yet another set of potential investors in the venture capital company he ran out of San Francisco. Drinks would be followed by a long, expensive and, he hoped, even more productive business dinner in a quiet corner of the elegant restaurant Jean-Georges near Lincoln Center.

Doing business was a fine way to spend a spring Saturday as far as Alex was concerned. Work was the only arena in which he felt comfortable. When he was at home in San Francisco he worked. When he traveled to New York or London or Taipei, he also worked. It was only during the little breaks between work that he felt on edge, jittery, bothered, too aware of the needs of his body and the permanent sense of loss in his heart.

Walking helped a little. Running would have helped more, but it would have meant two additional clothes changes and a shower before his five o'clock appointment. Too much time wasted. Suddenly bored with greenery, he headed west on Waverly Place toward the untidy bustle of Sixth Avenue. A couple of blocks north he crossed the street to get a closer look at the library, then went to the corner to wait for the walk light.

From that vantage point he watched shoppers cram their way into Balducci's, a specialty grocer, while others emerged, burdened and visibly harassed, from the exits.

His New York business acquaintances occasionally sent him gift baskets from the place. They sold several things Alex was crazy about—the most thinly cut smoked salmon in town, fresh cream cheese, a lemon tart that had had a walk-on role in one of his dreams and boxes of chocolate-chip cookies that were close enough to homemade to fool somebody like him, whose mother wasn't into cookies. He should go in, buy them out of those cookies and surprise his staff with them on Monday morning.

It really would be a surprise. He wasn't what you'd call a chocolate-chip-cookie kind of boss.

As this thought went through his mind, a woman came out of the shop carrying two of the distinctive green-and-white shopping bags. She set them down for a moment to set a brown leather handbag more firmly over her shoulder. She was reed-slim in narrow jeans, the dark-blue ones Alex had decided must be the fashion this spring. A loose white shirt floated over her arms, barely touching her body down to her waist where she'd tucked it in. High-heeled sandals added four inches to her already considerable height.

She was an extraordinarily striking woman. He felt drawn to her, a stranger, as he rarely felt drawn to the women who decorated his life as fleetingly as the bouquets of fresh flowers Burleigh routinely ordered for the round foyer table in Alex's Pacific Heights home. Just seeing her there gave him an oddly familiar surge of desire to penetrate a softness and warmth that felt too real to be a figment of his heated imagination.

She turned directly toward him for an instant, and he saw with the crystal clarity of cherished memories the fine skin, the blond hair that floated in the same ethereal fashion as her shirt, the generous mouth. His eyes opened wide. His lips parted. He breathed a single word.

"Sarah."

And then, as she took off like the Concorde, as comfortable on those high heels as if they'd been sneakers, he came to life. He couldn't shout her name. Men like him didn't shout women's names in public places. They didn't follow women up the street, either, but this was Sarah he was following, and he could not, would not, let her get away.

HURRYING NORTH, Sarah congratulated herself on how well the weekend was going. The evening before, she'd had drinks at the latest trendy bar—those ratings could change overnight—in Chelsea with Rachel and Annie, two friends from work. She'd chatted with an appealing man, an actor with a charming smile and high hopes, who'd auditioned the day before and had just gotten a callback.

A man for whom she had high hopes.

They'd agreed to meet for breakfast at a coffee shop in the West Village. He'd arrived with his lover, an equally appealing—but jealous—man.

However, while she waited for him, she'd shared the sports section of the *Times* with a better prospect, a lawyer with one of the city's large firms. They'd exchanged cards, and she fully expected to find a message from him on her answering machine when she got home. In the meantime, she'd prepared herself for whatever the evening—and the next morning—might bring.

Balducci's stocked a plentiful array of hors d'oeuvres and prepared foods, and she'd bought enough to manage dinner in case going out suddenly lost its charm. This afternoon she would make a dessert—a hazelnut torte, perhaps, or a flourless chocolate cake, or both.

She swung right onto Twelfth Street. Her bags also held bagels, smoked salmon, cream cheese and juice from apparently rare and valuable grapefruit, judging from the price. She would check the answering machine, then put her purchases away. Then, with everything in a state of readiness, she'd slip out onto the fire escape to let the sunshine and cool breeze arouse her to fever pitch. Her sixth sense told her the lawyer would be up to whatever level of passion she chose to demand of him.

She'd reached her building and started up the walk when she heard, "Sarah!" She froze, unable to move, unwilling to turn around. Her imagination was playing tricks on her, ugly, painful tricks. She heard footsteps behind her, and filled with dread, she slowly spun to face Alexander Asquith-Emerson, all grown-up.

"Sarah." He sounded out of breath. "It's Alex. Saw you coming out of Balducci's. It was just too amazing a coincidence." The rush of words coming from his mouth, a mouth that quirked up at one corner in an all-too-familiar way, suddenly halted.

Inside she was quaking so violently she was sure it showed on the outside. His hair was as thick and dark as ever, and his shoulders were broader in his well-tailored navy blazer than they'd been when he was eighteen. His eyes flashed dark, mysterious messages as they always had. An ache rose through her body that recalled the past even as it demanded recognition of the present.

"Fuhgeddaboudit," they said in Brooklyn. And, of course, she already had forgotten about it. A long time ago.

"Well. My goodness. After all these years. Alex Asquith-Emerson." Her spine felt like cold steel. She was proud of it for holding her up so firmly.

"Just Emerson." His full lower lip curved in a smile. "I dropped the Asquith. Too pretentious for the States."

His face held an expectant expression that frightened her. "Well," she said again, wishing she could bring her deceased vocabulary skills back to life. "It was good of you to go to all this trouble just to say hello."

"I didn't. Go to all this trouble just to say hello."

She waited, unable to move toward him or away from him. The ache had traveled up to her throat, making it impossible for her to answer.

"I've been trying to find you for years, Sarah. And suddenly, there you were."

He still had a faint trace of an upper-class English accent, and the rich quality of his voice had intensified with time. He had always been able to dissolve her with a word, merely her name spoken as only Alex could say it, but she was an adult now, immune to his manipulation.

"I've been here for the last five years," she said. "I own my own company. A graphics design firm." She wanted him to know she was in control of her own life and getting along just fine.

"I'm in and out of New York a lot. Wish I'd known you were here." He went on rapidly. "Well, now that I've found you we must get together sometime. I've filled up this weekend with business, I'm afraid, and have to head back home after lunch tomorrow..."

Sure, Alex, business.

"...but I'm coming back next weekend. Have dinner with me Friday night?"

I'd like to have you for dinner Friday night, you bastard. She forced breath into her lungs, forced her lips to move. "Sorry, I'm busy Friday."

"Saturday?"

"Busy Saturday, too. And I never go out on Sundays." She hoped he'd felt the point of the knife she'd just jabbed into him. "But it was great to see you." She turned away, longing for the safety and comfort of her own space, any space that didn't have Alex in it.

"Sarah."

The old deep, slow rhythm slowed her steps. She couldn't help herself.

"Here's my card. Call me if your plans change."

She took the card, tried to focus on it. She saw a San Francisco address. "You went back to California."

"Yes."

"Your mother?" She let her gaze rest on his face.

His wry smile added a touch of reality to the painful dream Sarah floated in. "In England. In excellent health, as impossible as ever and slowly killing husband number five. And your aunt Becki?"

The flood of sorrow rose inside her, as it always did. "She died. Eight years ago, while I was still in school."

"Oh, Sarah, I am sorry."

"Well." She gave him a bright, social smile as she gathered up her bags and started toward her doorway. She didn't know what she'd do if he followed her, offered to help with the bags, asked to come in. He didn't do any of those things. He just stood quietly, watching her.

"Enjoy your stay in New York," she said over her shoulder.

She got up the steps and through the doorway, fumbling with her keys. She made it to the tiny elevator at the end of the hall, to her apartment on the fifth floor and at last, to solitude.

Then she cried.

ROOTED TO THE SIDEWALK, Alex found it difficult to bend his knees.

As he watched Sarah vanish into the town house, he

felt as if his memories were burning him alive. Memories of the warm, silken feel of her stretched out over the full length of his body, or straddling him, clinging to his hair with her fingertips, or writhing beneath him, and finally lying quietly beside him, sated.

Suddenly edgy and needing to move around, he started slowly back toward Sixth Avenue. As soon as he'd officially reached adulthood and financial independence he'd begun searching for her, futilely trying to track her down through their mutual high-school friends, eventually surfing Internet telephone directories, state by state. She'd cut herself off, it seemed, vanished. He hadn't expected her to do that. He'd imagined she'd be there when the time was right. And today, at last, she'd appeared as if by magic.

It hadn't seemed possible. It still didn't seem possible.

He reached Sixth, stepped out onto the street and held up his hand. A taxi swerved, crossed two lanes and pulled up in front of him.

He wished the meeting had gone better, been easier, more comfortable, had given him some hope of forgiveness, yet he felt almost relieved by her hostility.

It meant she still cared.

"Hey, buddy, you want a cab or not?"

Alex gazed blankly through the window at the man, then climbed into the cab and tried desperately to restore his interest in the business deal that had seemed so important an hour ago.

2

"I WILL NOT BE spoken to in that tone," Jeremy said. His voice shook. "I know you're the boss, but it doesn't give you the right to be abusive. I have other options, Sarah. I turn down job offers right and left, higher pay, bigger assignments, because in the past—" he emphasized the words "—I have enjoyed working here." His chin quivered. "But I cannot work for a person who tells me my artwork has to be cremated before burial."

"Oh, Jeremy," Sarah said, genuinely remorseful. "I am so sorry." First Ray, now Jeremy. Jeremy was her ace computer-art person; she couldn't get along without him. She couldn't get along without any member of her small staff. Business was picking up as advertising agencies, in-house publicity departments and independent print salespeople grew familiar with her name and her product, but it was still a struggle to meet the overhead and pay salaries that were well below market. One glitch, one late delivery on a contract, one angry client taking his work elsewhere and she'd be bankrupt. Friendship and loyalty were all that kept these people with her, and she was alienating them one by one.

She slid her fingers through the silky waves of her hair, realizing that even her scalp itched. She felt feverish. She ached all over. But aspirin wasn't going to help. "I am not myself today."

"Or yesterday," Jeremy said. "Or three weeks ago Monday."

Sarah straightened up and spoke briskly. "I'm having a few personal problems," she said, "but it was both unkind and unprofessional of me to take it out on you. Please accept my apology."

"What about the artwork for the Designer Discounts mailer?" He eyed her suspiciously.

She cleared her throat. "I would appreciate it if you'd make one more stab at capturing the magic of a new shipment of Italian designer clothing."

"You mean the artwork stinks."

"In a manner of speaking."

He gave her a flashing smile. "Then why didn't you just say so?" He picked up the artwork and turned to leave Sarah's office. "Hey, Macon," he said as the two of them met in her doorway.

Sarah saw the significant glance that passed between them as Jeremy exited.

Macon came in, shut the door and sat down. "Well, you sure haven't gotten..."

"Don't say it!"

"Okay," Macon said, ever agreeable. "I'll put it another way. Your date Saturday night wasn't all you hoped and dreamed it would be."

"To say the least." Its hopes, disappointments and unexpected turns had left her hotter and more restless than ever.

"What happened?"

She fidgeted for a moment. "I couldn't."

"Couldn't what? I mean, if I were talking to a guy I'd know what he meant, but..."

Irritation increased the prickly sensations in her skin. "Macon," Sarah said. "When did you become my counselor? Who hired you? Who's paying you?"

"It's pro bono work," Macon said. "I'm not charging you a dime."

"Exactly what you're worth."

"Sarah, *what happened?*"

She couldn't sit still another minute. She swirled up and went to the windows of her office. They were filthy. Nothing unusual about that. The building management company wouldn't have them washed until a tenant threatened to write to the Housing Commission. From her eleventh-floor perch she could see through the grime a characteristically odd assortment of Chelsea rooftops. She saw water tanks and ventilation equipment surrounded by tarred surfaces already beginning to steam in the mild heat of spring. She saw elegant roof gardens, where trees and potted houseplants either flourished on their steady diet of toxic New York air or died, to be replaced at once by professional plant-maintenance crews. Nothing personal.

A Himalayan cat prowled among the expensive terracotta planters on one of the roofs, its long, pale hair fluffing up in the soft breeze. Maybe that was what she needed, a cat.

"What I *need* is a window-washer," she murmured.

"What?"

Her self-appointed counselor waited. In the middle of a fleeting daydream—the window-washer blowing kisses at her as he worked, her teasingly opening the window and watching as he came into her office, leaving no doubt in her mind that he was already aroused and

ready for her—Sarah suddenly realized there could be
no better repository for her anguished thoughts than the
compact mass of pure objective intelligence who was so
generously offering her his ear.

"I met a really promising prospect," she told him,
"but when the moment of reckoning arrived, I couldn't
go through with it."

"Tough scene to get through," Macon said, shaking
his head. "Frustrating for both of you."

"Unfair," she muttered, sinking back into her chair.
"And the worst part was that he was so nice about it."
He'd said he understood. He'd handed her his card with
an invitation to call anytime. Her life was filling up with
business cards. They made damned poor lovers.

She could tell from his expression that Macon couldn't
see why that had been the worst part. "I felt so guilty,"
she explained. "I really had led him on, with the *worst* of
intentions, of course."

"The question is why couldn't you go through with
it?"

A deep sigh rose all the way up from her tortured center. "Because earlier in the day I ran into the only man I
ever actually fell in love with."

"Wow," Macon said. "And he's married, right? Or an
ex-con. Or...Mafia!" His eyes lit up with interest, turning
his thick glasses into twin flashlight beams.

She gritted her teeth. "No, he's as perfect as ever."
Even more perfect, if that were possible. What a grim
thought.

"So you chased him down and he snubbed you." Macon looked properly outraged.

Sarah leapt up again and began to pace the confines of

the small, rose-walled office. The tension had built up so high inside her she felt as if she were about to come out of her skin. She could have asked Alex to come in. He would have come. One touch and she'd have led him to her bed. "He saw me, actually, and followed me home."

"Ha!" Macon said. "He's a—"

She spun. "No, he's not a stalker. He's..."

She had to gather up her courage to go on. "We were teenagers. He was my first lover. It was an experience so exquisite—" she halted, frightened by the threat of tears, by the impact of the memories that controlled her life even now "—I knew I wanted only that, with that person, for the rest of my life."

"And he *didn't?*"

Dear Macon. He couldn't believe a man she wanted would not want her. "I guess I wasn't good enough for him. At least, I wasn't good enough for his mother, the ever-so-famous movie star, and he didn't have the courage to defy her."

"You weren't good enough? Or your Aunt Becki wasn't the kind of..."

"Whatever," Sarah snapped. Of course she'd told Macon about Aunt Becki. She told everyone about Aunt Becki. Tall and blond like Sarah, but more beautiful than Sarah could ever dream of being, she'd been the mistress of a film producer, Todd Haynes. Although he had loved her deeply, he couldn't take the publicity of a divorce from his wife or the potential pain it would have caused his children.

Aunt Becki had loved him, too, so much that she'd been willing to accept what she could have of him. He'd provided her with a lovely little house in Beverly Hills, where he spent as much time as he could. And then, when Sarah's parents died, this cutthroat industry type had welcomed Sarah into that house as generously as Aunt Becki had, accepting without protest his mistress's need to shelter and comfort her sister's child.

Becki's and Todd's was a beautiful love story. Why anyone couldn't see how innately good Aunt Becki had been remained a mystery to Sarah, who'd been cared for with a kind of love Eleanor Asquith couldn't begin to understand.

"Hello in there," Macon said. "Where'd you go, Sarah?"

Sarah snapped to the present. "Alex and I were an item at Hollywood High. We made our plans. Pretty sensible plans, come to think of it, for a pair of kids drunk on love. He had to go to Cambridge—the Emerson men had been going to King's College for generations. I had a scholarship to Stanford. But we'd stay together, even if we were apart."

"This is so romantic it's making my scalp prickle."

"My scalp prickles, too, just thinking about it." The hollow sound of her voice came straight from the hollow feeling in her heart. "One night he just didn't show up, and I didn't see him again until last Saturday." She whirled on Macon again. "If you say, 'And how did that make you feel?' I'm going to shove you out the window."

Macon arranged his arms in a diving position. "See Macon," he said, "preparing to go gracefully."

ALEX SAT in glum silence in his stately suite of offices. Located in a historic old building in downtown San

Francisco, Emerson Associates was the venture capital firm he owned and had naively assumed he totally controlled. Apparently that assumption was incorrect. As far as he could tell, the offices were empty, which was odd, since it was Thursday. With a staff of five he managed hundreds of millions of dollars, which he then channeled into businesses that made the dollars thrive and multiply. He made sure those five people shared the success in salary increases, bonuses and stock shares. But in order for everyone to grow richer, those five people needed to show up at the office on a regular basis. Until today, they always had.

There was a fine, warm team spirit in the office. Especially when the team was in the damned office.

"Carol," he yelled.

Silence, followed by footsteps whose slow pace reeked of reluctance. A moment later a middle-aged, red-haired woman in a navy suit became visible by increments—the tip of her nose followed by the rest of her head, then a substantial bosom and, at last, a pair of surprisingly elegant legs. The whole package came to a halt just inside the doorway to his enormous office. He could barely see her at this distance.

"You called?"

Or hear her. "Of course I called. Where is everybody? Where's Mike with the Harbisher analysis? Where's..."

"Hiding," said Carol.

"What do you mean, hiding? Do we have a maniac loose in the office?"

"Yes."

"Carol," Alex said, forcing a tight smile, "come closer."

"Why?"

"Because I asked you! Nicely!"

She grabbed the door and closed it silently, his shout echoing against it.

"So much for nicely," he muttered. His single objection to his staff was that they didn't always treat him with the respect he, as owner of the firm, properly deserved. They treated him more like family. A *younger* member of the family, to add to the insult. So what if he was thirty years old, younger than anybody, except the office manager? Didn't matter. This was his castle and he should be king.

Of course, they were Americans. They took a dim view of kings. That might explain it.

For a few minutes he remained at his desk, fuming. Then, being a man of action, he got up and went in search of his people.

He found them huddled together in Mike's office. Mike Semple was his financial analyst. Carol, his executive assistant, was just sitting down at Mike's conference table with Suzi, the office manager, Les, his management analyst and Tricia, negotiator and director of communications.

"Good of you to join us, Alex," Mike said. "We were just starting a staff meeting."

"Without me?" Alex felt startled and oddly unbalanced.

"About you."

"Oh." Alex nudged Suzi to the left and Les to the right in order to plunk himself down in a side chair, avoiding his usual spot at the head of the table. "Good thing I showed up. What is it about me we're discussing?"

"We're wondering what's up," Les said. "Are we going broke?"

"No."

"Did we underbid for Palmer Pipe Company?"

"No. Look, I know I haven't been in the best mood the last couple of days." To his annoyance, his team answered him not with reassurance, but with, to be precise, two nervous giggles and three derisive snorts. "It's a personal matter," he said, hoping that those sacred words would end this ridiculous cross-examination as it would in any civilized sort of setting. Americans, however, were not yet completely civilized, as he had learned from numerous painful experiences. They talked too openly about matters they should keep to themselves, and in return, wanted the most outrageously intimate details from others. You'd think, with more than two hundred years of practice, they'd learn to stop asking how much you made in a year. And whom you were sleeping with. At least one of the two.

"I didn't know you had any personal matters," Suzi said.

Of course, Suzi was still very young.

"I didn't know you had any personal anything," Les seconded her. "Except your toothbrush."

Now Les should have known better than to mention something as personal as a toothbrush.

"Put the problem on the table," Mike suggested. "We'll discuss it just like we discuss business problems."

As his senior person, Mike should be hanged for what he'd just said. This was not fine, warm team spirit. This was insubordination of the most outrageous, most insupportable nature. He wouldn't put up with it. He'd fire the lot of them. Let them find somebody else to work for, somebody who could increase their net worths by eighty percent annually instead of a mere seventy.

He suddenly heard himself, his irritability, his childishness. He had plenty of faults, but childishness wasn't one of them. He hadn't been childish even when he was a child. His mother hadn't allowed it. So why was it suddenly showing up now?

It must have been the distraction of his own thoughts that made him blurt out the one thing he most wanted to keep to himself. Either that, or he'd lived in the United States too long. "I ran into an old girlfriend in New York last weekend."

That was as far as he got before a collective sigh drowned him out, followed by, "No kidding?" and "Great!" and "Uh-oh, it's a woman problem."

"I told you it had to be something important," Suzi said. "Tell us all about her."

Cornered by his own stupidity, Alex said, "No, no, it's not like that. She's just a girl I dated in high school. Hollywood High. When my mother did those three movies—" He made a gesture with his hand. He didn't need to embellish. Eleanor Asquith was a household name, in cultured households, at least. "She pulled me out of boarding school and brought me with her. She wanted me to see what real Americans were like."

"Real Americans at Hollywood High? I don't *think* so," Les said.

"Sarah was there."

The silence told him he'd shocked them. It was a frightening thought, that he might have said more than one of them would have in the same circumstances. What was it that made him babble on? "We fell for each other, but this and that happened, you know how it is with kids, and we broke up. I lost track of her. Last Saturday I found her again."

"Something about this reunion did not make you happy." Mike folded his hands over an incipient paunch and waited.

Alex had opened the doors himself. There was no going back. "I thought it would be the polite thing to ask her out this weekend. She turned me down flat. I gave her my card and asked her to call if her plans changed."

"I didn't know you were going to New York this weekend," Carol said, looking worried. "You loaned the plane to Tucker Associates, remember? You don't have transportation or a hotel suite, and you don't have any appointments."

"Well, *obviously*," Alex began, then, realizing he sounded sarcastic, backed up and started over. "I wasn't going to New York unless she called."

"But she didn't call," Suzi said.

"Not yet."

"It's only...well, I guess it *is* Thursday," Mike said. "Looks like maybe she's not going to call." He winced under the glare Alex sent in his direction.

"She calls or she doesn't," Alex said. "It doesn't matter. I'm annoyed by her bad manners, that's all."

"If you did something to make her so mad that she's still mad after all these years," Suzi said, "it may take her more than five days to get over it."

"Or maybe you need to push her a little bit," Carol suggested. "If this was a business deal you wouldn't let it go with a single, 'Let's take a meeting,' and then just sit around on your tush waiting for the other guy to call."

"If this was a business deal," Suzi said, echoing Carol, "you'd put together a package for the guy, an annual report, a prospectus, your card, maybe an Emerson Associates paperweight."

A lightbulb went off in Alex's head. *A business deal. Of course.* It was a road toward Sarah, and it was a way out of the untenable social predicament he'd gotten himself into with his staff. "In fact, it was a business deal I had in mind," he said smoothly. He let his fingers stray casually toward the most recent prospectus he'd sent to a group of potential investors. It was shiny, glossy, colorful, printed on heavy, expensive paper, filled with photographs, the essential charts and graphs cleverly disguised by their Disneylike style. "This—" he brandished it at them "—didn't really send the message, did it?"

He looked up when silence seemed to be the only response he was going to get.

"I was thinking we should tell the ad agency to look for a new graphics design firm. Somebody with a fresh, quirky approach might make the difference, tip the scale."

Meaningful glances sizzled around the table. "Can we infer," Mike said in his most pompous tone, "that the lady works for a graphics design firm?"

"Owns it," Alex informed them, and couldn't keep the tinge of pride out of his voice.

With nothing more than graphics design and New York to go on, he'd found her on the Internet earlier in the week. At least he'd found the person who had to be Sarah. She'd been Sarah Langley way back then; when her aunt adopted her after her parents' death, she'd taken Aunt Becki's last name. Now she was Sarah Nevins, her father's name, and the sole owner of Great Graphics! in Chelsea. Five employees. Undercapitalized, barely making it, but getting good feedback on their work.

The search had made him feel like a cyberstalker, and he didn't intend to share anything but the firm's name, even with these people.

"Oh, for heaven's sake," Suzi said, interrupting his thoughts. "I meant send flowers."

She so obviously wanted to add "You turkey," that in spite of his annoyance that she still wasn't listening, Alex couldn't help but admire her restraint. "Flowers wouldn't be appropriate," he argued. "A contract to do our brochures and stuff, now that's an offer she couldn't refuse."

Thinking of Sarah not refusing him was enough to make him shift discreetly in his chair. He could hardly say her name without getting hard, and picturing her lying soft, sweet and naked in his bed, saying, "Yes, oh, yes..."

"Oh, yes," he said firmly, "a big contract will make an impression on her."

More silence. "Could we try it my way first?" Suzi pleaded with him.

"I'd vote for that," Mike said. "Or candy."

"How many times do I have to tell you. This is a business..." Alex said.

"Candy's risky," Les said. "Give my wife candy, she says, 'You want me fat so you can run off with some skinny bimbo?'"

"What would she say to a fat contract?" Alex inquired.

Their sympathetic, patronizing expressions spoke volumes. "Who's our florist of choice these days, Suzi?" Carol said succinctly.

"THIS ISN'T COMPANY BUSINESS," Sarah snapped. "You don't get to address my personal life in a staff meeting."

Each of her loyal colleagues handed her a sheet of paper. She glanced down at the first, which was from Ray. A letter of resignation. Her hands began to tremble as she leafed through one sheet after the other.

"You're all resigning?"

"Or," Macon said, "we're going to discuss your personal life in this staff meeting."

"Blackmail."

"Right."

"What precipitated this...mutiny?"

They all spoke at once.

"The last grain of sand..." Macon began.

"The straw that broke the camel's back..." Rachel said.

"The lowest blow..." Ray said.

"The final blow..." Annie said, sounding teary, "was when you told me my Citibank brochure would make great confetti for the Macy's Thanksgiving Day parade."

"It was...*vivid*," Sarah said. "It was hard to imagine bank customers relating Mardi Gras to estate planning." She had to establish control over this situation. "But I apologize for my choice of words."

"Your vocabulary has blossomed over the last few days," Jeremy said. "We think it's time to deadhead it."

"That was very good, Jeremy," Sarah said, "that connection between *blossoming* and *deadheading*."

"What's deadheading?" said Rachel, whose idea of country life was to visit the Brooklyn Botanical Gardens. "It sounds more sadistic than I, *personally*, feel at the moment."

"It was a metaphor," Macon said impatiently. "Jeremy was drawing a nice little metaphor, which surprised Sarah because he's the artist and Ray's the writer and..."

"You're killing it with analysis," Annie interrupted him.

"Thank you, Annie," Macon said. "The point, Sarah," he went on, "is that you're obviously unhappy, and if you won't do something about it, we're moving on."

"Like wagons at dawn," Sarah said, gazing at them sorrowfully, "leaving the sick and wounded behind."

"You got it," Ray said. "Now on the other hand, if you would lend a receptive ear, we might suggest a cure."

If Ray offered to solve her problem as Macon had, she'd scream. It was unlikely, given that Ray and Jeremy were a couple. "My, my, the rhetoric is just flowing this afternoon," Sarah said. "If only we could put this same creative effort into our *copywriting*, Ray, we might..."

"You're doing it again," Jeremy warned her.

Sarah waved both hands in the air, noticing sadly that they flinched. "I'm turning down your resignations. Okay, what do you think I should do?"

"Call him," Annie said.

They didn't understand. "I can't, Annie, I just can't. What he did to me..."

"About a million years ago," Jeremy interjected.

"I take it Macon has given you the gist of the story."

"It was the only way he could talk us out of e-mailing our resignations and sneaking back in the dark of night to clear out our desks," Rachel said.

"Oh. Then I suppose I should say thank you," Sarah said, turning to Macon.

"It would be a change."

Her grudging smile segued at once into a glower. "Okay, okay, it was twelve years ago, I admit, and I was dealing with it just fine until I saw him again. Well, I was," she retorted, reacting to the expressions on their faces.

"But now that you *have* seen him again," Rachel argued, "you're going to have to resolve your feelings about him."

"Or you'll resign," Sarah said, feeling sulky.

"Or you'll explode," Jeremy said.

"Or implode," Ray said.

"I wouldn't mind if she'd *im*plode," Jeremy said. "It's the *ex*ploding that's making me think that job with Hall & Lindstrom wouldn't be such a bad idea."

"Jeremy, you wouldn't!"

"Sarah," he mimicked her, "I would and will if you don't..."

"...call him," her five devoted employees chorused while Sarah glared at them.

SHE WOULDN'T. She couldn't. They didn't understand.

That summer, the summer after she and Alex graduated, they were more desperate for each other than ever, knowing that soon they'd be going away to college. They would be apart in body, but not in spirit. They would work it out. What they had was too perfect to let go.

No one could imagine how she felt the night she waited for him, hot and tremulous, already wet and ready for him just knowing she would see him in a few minutes. It was agony to act normal in front of Aunt Becki. But this time Alex simply didn't arrive. No letter, no phone call, no Alex. Not ever again.

Her knees buckled as she went up the steps to her building. Gritting her teeth against the pain she'd managed to keep in a separate compartment of her soul for so many years, Sarah turned the key in the lock, heard the reassuring click and pushed at the main door, surprised when very little happened. She shoved a little harder.

"Don't knock over the flowers!" It was her first-floor neighbor Maude who shouted at her from her apartment window. While Sarah hesitated, a door slammed, indicating that Maude had come out into the narrow entrance hall. A series of mutters followed, alternating with oofs and grunts. "You think I have nothing better to do than sign for your deliveries, collect your menus from Chinese restaurants? Where's my big Christmas tip, that's what I'd like to know."

Maude, being a writer and a famous one at that, worked at home, and so, by default, was the building's doorperson. Her diatribes on this subject were long, loud and venomous.

"Sorry, Maude. What flowers?"

"*Your* flowers," Maude said. "So stop trying to break down the door until I get them shoved out of the way."

The staff had sent flowers to cheer her up, let her

know they didn't really hate her. How sweet of them. They shouldn't be spending their money, what little they had of it, this way. The door suddenly burst open and Sarah fell into a virtual conservatory.

If not quite a conservatory, it was certainly an enormous bouquet, largely composed of white orchids whose long streamers of blossoms waved toward the high ceiling of the entry. The vase wasn't a standard florist's container, but a frosty-looking piece of handblown glass in a pale, smoky hue. Sarah gazed at it, feeling stunned.

"How're you going to get it into the elevator?" Maude said. Her expression was sour. Beside her, a doleful basset hound uttered a soft moan.

Sarah's ears buzzed and her voice seemed to come from a distance. "I can't imagine. Call the Longshoreman's Union and see if somebody wants a job on the side?"

"I've got a dolly." The words dripped out as slowly as liquid through an intravenous tube.

"Why, thank you, Maude. Just give me a sec to read the card."

If she wasn't mistaken, the cardholder that feathered up through the orchids was crafted in sterling silver. Her entire staff put together didn't have that much money to spare. She knew what the card would say even before she opened the tiny envelope:

Dear Sarah:
Sorry this weekend didn't work out for you. How about next weekend? You can reach me at any of these numbers....

Her eyes blurred on the string of numbers, written in the neat hand of someone at the florist's shop, not in a large, rounded scrawl. If the card had actually been in the handwriting she remembered so well as being distinctively Alex's, she might have fainted.

3

What a gorgeous bouquet! Thanks so much. It was far too large for my apartment, so I put it on the table in the front hall where all the tenants in my building could enjoy it.

It was very nice to see you again. Unfortunately, I won't be in town next weekend. I have a new client in...

Sarah halted, her pen poised, thinking of unlikely, out-of-the-way places Alex wouldn't dream of suggesting he join her. It wasn't easy. In spite of his wealth and sophistication, Alex had his own interesting way of fitting in everywhere, seemingly as relaxed at the small round table in Aunt Becki's cottage or eating hamburgers in a greasy spoon as he was in the massive dining room of Eleanor Asquith's Bel Air mansion.

It was called noblesse oblige, or you could call it plain good manners.

Extensive travel with his mother and her entourage had made him flexible. He could handle cold weather, hot weather and rainy season in the tropics, mountains, deserts and forests.

One thing he hated was inconvenience. Waiting. He liked his trains to run on time, so to speak. So...where could you almost not get to from San Francisco? Someplace you might not choose to go in the first place.

It struck her that Dubuque, Iowa, might be the perfect solution. A quick Internet check showed her that although Dubuque wasn't impossible to reach from San Francisco, it could not be reached very directly.

> *...in Dubuque, Iowa, and must make a trip there on Friday. Perhaps another time.*
> *Again, thank you for the magnificent bouquet.*
>> *Most sincerely,*
>> *Sarah*

She paused again, then added "Nevins." Alex would read her message— "shove off" —loud and clear in her formal language and the use of her last name. He liked getting his own way, yes, but he also had an inner dignity that would keep him from pushing.

Not daring to give herself time to think it over, she licked the envelope flap, pounded it down with her fist, slapped on a stamp and raced for the corner mailbox.

She'd waited until morning to decide how to react to Alex's floral offering, and felt she'd handled it well. As she sauntered back to her building, she saw that a crew had arrived to do their annual maintenance to the carefully preserved slate roof of the nineteenth-century town house.

At least her apartment house was managed by a responsible, sensitive building management firm, quite unlike the skinflints who managed her office building. She paused for a moment to admire the broad, muscled back and spectacular buns of the man who was directing his workers to the back of the building where a scaffolding was already in place. Wouldn't it be great if she could lure him into her home for a brief interlude before her own workday started?

It was one thing to entertain such a delightful thought, and quite another to emerge from the shower a short time later and see a man's face looking through her bathroom window.

Sarah opened her mouth to scream. The neighborhood had been plagued by a Peeping Tom in the last few years. Maude, who claimed to have sighted him twice, had warned her to keep her windows closed and locked and her shades down as the scaffolding provided such easy access to all floors of the building, but had Sarah listened? No, and here she was, facing the Village Voyeur himself!

"Whoa!" the man said through the open window, just before her scream emerged.

She clutched her bath sheet tighter and glared at him. "What do you think you're doing, looking in my..."

All of a sudden she realized she was seeing the front of the very man whose back she'd been admiring earlier. He gave her a broad, brilliant smile and tipped the bill of his cap. "I'm the roofing contractor, ma'am. Don't mind me. I'm just on my way up."

His words trailed off as his gaze focused directly on her. The scene took on the misty quality of a romantic movie as she gazed back. Tall, dark, handsome, deeply tanned—and he was a roofing contractor. Perfect, simply perfect.

Before the fantasy ended, they'd made a date to go out for Thai food that very night. By nine o'clock that evening she wished she *had* remembered to pull the shades down. The roofing contractor might be breathtakingly handsome, but he was not going to become her man-for-the-moment. Not even for a split second. He told terrible jokes terribly, quizzed the waiter relentlessly until he was sure he hadn't ordered any Thai food that had any Thai seasonings in it, and she had a deep-seated suspicion he'd neglected to mention he was married. His line, delivered in a low, sexy voice while his eyelids drooped in a manner he must have thought was suggestive, was: "How about we head up to your apartment for a quick one before I hit the road to Brooklyn."

As the word *Brooklyn* came across the table, Sarah conceded that the misty quality of their accidental morning meeting was entirely due to steam from the shower. "I don't drink after dinner," she said, then added, "Tonight's my treat." She whipped out her billfold.

"I wasn't talking drinks, foxy lady, I was talking..."

Foxy lady? Bleah-h-h-h. She knew perfectly well a drink was not the "quick one" he had in mind. She handled the transaction so swiftly, estimating the tip, rounding it off on the high side and paying in cash, that she was off in one direction and he in another before he had time to absorb the situation.

Not that she was giving up on the idea of finding a man. She would demand to have her office windows washed at once or the management company could look for a new tenant.

She said as much to Annie on Monday morning after a frustrating, unproductive weekend. A worried look came over Annie's face.

"Uh, I'll tell them that, but it'll be an empty threat."

"How so?" She strongly felt the management company owed her a crew of muscled hunks, just for letting the windows go for such a long time.

"You can't afford to move."

She knew it, of course, but Annie's expression told her there were other things she needed to know. In addition to supplementing Jeremy's design work, Annie kept the Great Graphics! books.

"What's our financial situation?"

"I don't know how you're going to meet the payroll next month."

"That bad?" Sarah's other frustrations fled as a sick feeling settled into the pit of her stomach. "Well, for starters, I won't pay myself. I can manage for a while."

Macon stuck his head through the doorway. "I can manage for...well, forever, I guess."

"Oh, Macon," Sarah said, "I pay you little enough as it is."

"But you let me keep my consulting business. I've been making money working with computers since I was thirteen," he told her, "and apparently not spending it." He frowned, as if he were wondering what on earth other people did with their money. "Except on more computer equipment."

"We can take it a month at a time," Annie said, giving the printout of her spreadsheet a steel-eyed gaze. "If you two can forgo salaries next month, I'll lean on the Zweig Company for the money they still owe us, and if that doesn't do it, we can hit Ray and Jeremy up for the next month." She gave Sarah an apologetic look. "Rachel and I are both living right on the edge as it is."

"We will not 'hit up' anybody else," Sarah said. "I've

got to get out there and drum up more business." She
didn't miss the sidelong glance that passed between Macon and Annie. They already had all the work they could
do, but the jobs were small ones with a low-profit mar-
gin. She was in deep trouble, and at the moment, lacked
the necessary backbone to get herself out of it.

IT SEEMED NOTHING SHORT of a miracle to learn that the
window-washers had arrived at the office building.
Sarah found it particularly annoying to pick up the telephone just as she was looking over the crew and find
Alex on the other end of the line.

Rachel was a wonderful office manager and general
factotum, but the announcement, "Guy on the phone
wants to talk to you about some work," was not the sort
of briefing one needed before speaking with the enemy.

"Sarah. Hello."

Sarah took a deep breath. He must have lied to Rachel,
and she wasn't going to let him get away with it.

"Alex." *Well done.* She was as cool as a mint Lifesaver.
"Did I pick up on the wrong line? Rachel said a potential
client was calling."

"That's me. Alex Emerson, potential client."

She blinked. "Oh. Well. What can I do for you?" *Or to
you, you scum on a picture postcard English pond.*

"Actually, the reason I've been so persistent about
dinner," Alex said, "is that I have a project I want to talk
to you about."

He'd said the magic word. "A project?"

"Yes. My promotional materials. I don't like the product I'm getting now. I've told the ad agency to contract
the work to somebody different, but I've been asking

around myself, too, and somebody mentioned your name. Said he'd been happy with your work."

"Who?"

"Si Harper. The guy at Super Shuttle. That's the new airline that runs shuttles from New York to..."

"I know Si. I know what Super Shuttle does." She hoped he hadn't heard her gasp. How had he found out she did Super Shuttle's work?

"Carol, my person here, tells me I can take the company jet as far as the Midway Airport..."

She hadn't been thinking. Of course he would have his own plane. No place on earth was too inconvenient for Alex to reach.

"...but I can't land it in Cedar Rapids. The private strip is closed for construction. So I'll take a taxi to O'Hare, get on a United shuttle to Cedar Rapids, then rent a car and drive up to Dubuque."

When he mentioned O'Hare, Sarah felt tempted. As a hub of air travel for the continental United States, Chicago's O'Hare was a wonderfully chancy airport. An electrical storm on either coast and O'Hare came to a standstill. If she had a thousand dollars for each person she knew personally who'd had to spend a night in that airport, she'd have the down payment for a two-bedroom apartment. She relished the image of Alex stretched out on waiting-room seats, only half-covered by a scratchy gray airline blanket, a thread of mozzarella from his dinner—a slice of cold pizza—hanging from the corner of his mouth.

That was the other thing Alex hated—the loss of his dignity.

But Alex would consume a slice of cold pizza in the

same graceful way he did everything else, without drooling, and if he absolutely had to sleep, he'd do it sitting up. Without snoring. Besides, with her luck, he'd probably arrive in Dubuque without incident, only to find out she was a liar.

"I've cancelled the trip to Dubuque," she admitted. A brainstorm struck. "I convinced the customer there was really no need for a face-to-face meeting. We can handle everything fine by phone and e-mail." She warmed to her theme. "Just as I can handle your account, if you're serious about needing to have some work done."

In the brief silence that ensued she imagined she could hear Alex thinking. Instead, she heard, "Forget Dubuque, Carol," and then, "Oh, I'm very serious. But the design firm our ad agency has been using has the same attitude you just described, and I'm more of a hands-on person."

How well she knew that. His hands-on policy had awakened her to sensations she could never have dreamed of, to pure, hot, insistent...

"I was hoping your firm might take a more personal approach to your clients."

"We do, of course," Sarah said. "We want to be sensitive to our clients' perceived needs and self-images." She trailed off, distracted by an odd echo on the line.

"I have very strong feelings about my investors, the companies I invest in and everything that goes out under my name. I require periodic face-to-face discussions, whether I'm buying or selling. It means a lot of travel, but it's worth it," he said.

"I see."

"I'd insist on an initial meeting at the very least."

"What's your print budget?" It was a rude question, but he was gaming her, dangling a carrot in front of her nose, and she needed to know how sweet that carrot was before she bit into it.

"A million and a quarter, give or take."

With great difficulty Sarah kept herself from saying, "Dollars?"

Now she faced a new distraction. Jeremy crept into her doorway and mouthed, "Take it!" Ray moved up behind Jeremy, nodding vigorously. Annie thrust herself between them, giving Sarah a pleading expression complete with a Virgin-Mary-clasped-hands pose. There wasn't room in the doorway for anyone else. Rachel had clearly left the line open and the speakerphone on, and the whole staff was begging her not to turn down a plum contract simply because she was too chicken to see Alex Emerson again.

They *did* work for peanuts. Their deal with her contained no definition of overtime and therefore no compensation for it. And still, cutting every corner, the firm was barely keeping its head out of the minestrone.

She owed them this contract. And to get it, she'd have to get it on Alex's terms. The customer, damn him, was always right.

"I suppose one meeting would..."

Victory signals came at her from the doorway. She frowned.

"...get the basics worked out."

A hand, either Macon's or Rachel's, shot through the doorway to wave a small American flag with a white hanky of peace tied to it.

"Saturday, then. At seven."

She hung up slowly. The breeze from the collective sigh of relief that emerged from the doorway lifted the tendrils of hair off her suddenly hot forehead.

SARAH EYED HERSELF in the full-length mirror in her bedroom, turned to the left, then to the right. After, she picked up a hand mirror to get a rear view.

This wasn't the right dress, either. It would be the fourth dress she'd brought home and taken back.

She knew she wasn't behaving rationally, but self-awareness was a long way off from behavior modification and she didn't have time to travel that road.

Curse Alex and his British correctness. Of course, he would insist on picking her up and bringing her home. She could protest until she turned blue that the modern woman was perfectly capable of getting herself to and from a restaurant, but her reasoning wouldn't work on Alex.

So she'd volunteered to make dessert.

Now why the hell had she done that?

Because Alex would insist on paying for dinner, and the only way she could strike back was to offer dessert, coffee and brandy.

Because Alex had a legendary sweet tooth.

Because by the sheerest coincidence, desserts were the only cooking she did, and she'd gotten pretty good at doing them.

Sarah buried her face in her hands. Dusk was falling on this Thursday night in early June. The wedge of sky she could glimpse through her bedroom window was such a thrilling mix of terracotta pink and orange, it seemed irreverent to think of it as merely pollution from a million cars crossing bridges, threading through tunnels on their way to the New Jersey and Connecticut suburbs.

That's what she'd like to do—leave town. Instead, she had to get back to Loehmann's before it closed, return the dress, then scour the grocery and specialty stores for dessert ingredients.

The cold lump in her stomach grew larger. Which dessert? Crème brûlée for sure.

A memory drifted through her mind, sharp, clear and bittersweet—Aunt Becki making crème brûlée for her lover, just in case he might be able to come to dinner that night.

"What do you think, sweetheart?" she could hear Aunt Becki saying in her sweet, laughing voice. "Have I got it? A little browner, do you think, or is it just right?"

Todd had not been able to break free from his family and come to dinner that night. "It was good practice," Aunt Becki declared, as cheerful as ever, although her glow had dimmed a little. "Let's try it out on Alex when he picks you up tonight. See what he thinks. He probably knows exactly what a crème brûlée should be."

Alex had licked his lips over the crunchy broiled brown-sugar top and the creamy interior of the dessert and pronounced it to be the model against which all other crème brûlée should be measured. At Aunt Becki's insistence, he'd taken one home to Burleigh, the butler who'd been like a father to fatherless Alex, a man who'd seen, heard, experienced and eaten everything in his position with the formidable Eleanor Asquith, Lady Forsythe at the time Sarah met her.

She wished she'd asked Alex how Burleigh was.

Slowly her attention returned to the immediate problem. Maybe she didn't want to remind Alex of the past. Personally, she was hungry for an almond zuger kirschtorte, layers of fluffy white cake baked with meringue on top and put together with tons of buttercream frosting.

Some people didn't like cake.

Or a clafoutis. Alex could watch her stir up the batter and pour it over the fruit, and while it baked they could...

Scratch the clafoutis.

Some people didn't think it was dessert unless it was chocolate. The warm chocolate cake would present the same timing problem as the clafoutis, the timing problem being time alone with Alex. Her fudge pecan pie would cover the chocolate front.

On the other hand, Alex might have developed an allergy to chocolate.

She groaned. First, Loehmann's.

THE SOUND OF THE BUZZER set Sarah's heart to pounding painfully. Her hand shook as she picked up the house phone. "It's Alex," he said, as if she might not recognize his voice.

What she could do was simply not push the button that unlocked the front door. Then she could go out the back window and down the fire escape, grab a taxi on Sixth Avenue, go to a car rental agency and leave for someplace cool, quiet and Alex-free. Like the Yukon.

"Come on up. Fifth floor," she heard herself say, then watched herself push the button.

After hanging up, she stared at the phone. Then she heard a knock at the door.

"Sarah." He was there too soon, filling her living room with his size and strength, with the power he still held over her. "For you." He handed her an armful of apricot-colored roses with lush, heavy heads still tightly closed.

Sarah cast a nervous glance around the room, noting all its peachy-apricot accents, wondering if he'd known, how he'd known. "Thank you," she murmured. "They're beautiful. Just let me..."

She was grateful to have an excuse to flee to the kitchen. She stuck the roses into the biggest container she could find—a crystal ice bucket she'd inherited from Aunt Becki that was large enough to chill champagne for a small party. Taking a deep breath, she went back to Alex.

She found him gazing slowly around her living room with its cream walls, the pale-blue ceiling she'd painted herself. "So this is where you live," he said. "It looks so much like—"

"Aunt Becki's cottage," she interrupted him.

"Yes. I always felt good there."

The unexpected words stopped her in her nervous, darting tracks, the vase filled with roses still clutched in her hands. "You did?"

"More comfortable than I felt anywhere else." He reached out a hand and touched the lace that bordered one of the many pillows on the sofa, which was slipcovered in a fabric Aunt Becki herself might have chosen, a faded floral pattern of blues, greens, and apricot colors, similar to those of the roses Alex had given her, against a cream background. Had he remembered? Had he chosen the roses because they reminded him of the past?

She put the roses on a small antique table, forcing herself to speak naturally. "I felt good there, too. When she died, Todd—" She broke off. "Did you ever meet Todd Haynes? Aunt Becki's—"

"Friend," Alex said. He hesitated. "Yes. Once. He came to our house for dinner."

Alex had never told her this. "But not with Aunt Becki, I imagine." She managed a smile.

Again, he spoke reluctantly, but seemed determined to be honest. "No. With his wife. Haynes produced one of Mother's movies. Mother and his wife saw each other at industry parties and had become friends."

Eleanor Asquith must have known about Todd's long-standing relationship with Becki Langley. Aunt Becki had not merely been a kept woman, but "the other woman" in Eleanor's eyes. But hadn't Eleanor Asquith been "the other woman" often enough herself?

This was a business dinner she was having with Alex. It wasn't in her best interests to start off angry. "I see," she said. "Well, anyway, Todd insisted on giving me everything that had been hers. I put it in storage, and when I was settled here, I sent for it."

"It suits the room."

The rooms of her apartment were tiny but high-ceilinged. This one was a twelve by twelve by twelve-foot box. Aunt Becki's pretty, feminine things did suit the room, and had made Sarah feel instantly at home, as well.

"It suits you, too."

For a minute she thought he was about to move toward her. Instead, he glanced out one window at the fire escape, where an exuberance of purple and white petunias bloomed beside pots of geraniums with salmon-colored blossoms. He smiled, and went to the tall, narrow front windows. "The street's so quiet you'd never know you were in Manhattan," he said.

"The burglar bars on the house across the street might give you a clue."

He flashed a different kind of smile at her, and she felt that he was pulling himself back from memories of the past, just as she was. "Who's the gorgon you've got guarding the door down there?"

Gorgon? "Oh, you must have met Maude. Maude Coates."

"*The* Maude Coates? Who writes the thrillers?"

"The very same."

"Damn. I'm reading her latest book. I could've gotten her autograph. She scared the hell out of me. Thought I was going to get bitten. I gave her half the roses I was bringing to you as a peace offering."

"Was Broderick with her?"

"The depressed-looking basset hound?"

"That's Broderick. Named for Broderick Crawford, not Matthew Broderick. Broderick wouldn't dream of biting anybody."

"Wasn't Broderick I was afraid of."

Wasn't Broderick she was afraid of, either. Alex was too handsome in his dark suit, too charming. She had to keep her guard up, have nothing on her mind except getting this contract into her life and Alex out of it.

STAY CALM. DON'T SCARE HER. She was like a bowstring drawn back so tightly that one jostle and the arrow would fly—straight for his chest.

She wore a short black dress with a small white jacket. On her feet, sandals, nothing more than shiny little black straps on skyscraper heels. Her toenails were pink. No stockings. The heat that consumed him just by imagining the small pair of panties she'd be wearing under the silky dress was almost more than he could handle. He wondered if, under that jacket, the dress looked like a slip. Was there anything between it and the small, perfectly shaped breasts he remembered so well?

Get a grip. Don't obsess.

He frowned at his watch. "Ready to go? We'll have a drink and then go on to dinner."

"Would you rather have a drink here?"

Hell, yes, I'd rather, and dinner here, or just skip all that and...

"They're holding a table for me in the Regency bar," he said, quashing his baser instincts. "We can spread out our work, set up a laptop. My briefcase is in the car. Where's yours?"

He thought she flushed a little. He didn't see a briefcase anywhere in the living room, just a small black handbag. If she'd forgotten that tonight was meant to be a business meeting, wouldn't that be just won—

"Right here," she said. The angelic cloud of wavy blond hair floated around her shoulders as she leaned down to a spot beside the flowered sofa.

"Right. Off we go."

OVER DRINKS ALEX EXPLAINED his immediate needs for publicity materials. His account executive at the ad agency had outlined everything for him and would work with Sarah on the details.

Couldn't she just have gone directly to the agency?

It was hard to concentrate with Alex there beside her. He didn't seem bothered or distracted at all. Maybe business was all he'd had in mind from the beginning. That would be a relief. Or would it?

The silk of her dress brushed against her breasts each time she leaned forward to make a point. Her nipples felt tight, tingly.

"Our dinner reservation's at eight-thirty," Alex said abruptly. "I think we've accomplished a lot here, don't you?"

"Yes, yes," Sarah said breathlessly. "I have a very clear idea of what you want."

The only very clear idea she had was about what she wanted, and she couldn't have it. She couldn't let herself have it, even if it was hers for the taking.

He took her to dinner at Le Perigord, a midtown neighborhood restaurant. The food was delicious, the service a wonderful combination of elegance and chatty friendliness. It wasn't exactly a candlelit house of seduction, but a man like Alex didn't need candlelight.

"Where did you go after you left Stanford?" he asked, while she nibbled on her main course.

It was an innocent enough question. It was also like Alex to skip the painful years and move right into appropriate dinner conversation. It was the way he gazed at her across the table, his dark eyes seeming to ask her deeper questions, that made anything he said unsettling.

"I'd always been interested in graphic design," she said, matching his tone, "so I took one job after another until I felt I'd learned my trade, then came here and started my business with what was left of my inheritance and what I'd saved. I've been lucky," she added, suddenly realizing she had been.

She'd also been in great demand. Each job had brought a higher salary, but she saw no reason to share those things with him. Success and wealth were things he took for granted. He would easily understand that while her business could be called successful, her overhead was enormous and the cash flow situation had currently reached the crisis point. That was his job. What he would never understand was how much it meant to her to make a go of this business, because it had all come so easily to him.

"What made you decide to change your name, vanish so completely?"

The question took her by surprise, forced her to give him a quick glance. His gaze, always compelling, had intensified until she felt she might drown in it.

"I'd had a lot of sadness," she said abruptly, "losing my parents and then Aunt Becki. I wanted to be a different person, I guess, without any links to the past."

"I'm sorry for my contribution to your sadness."

His voice was soft, but somehow the cheerful, noisy atmosphere of the restaurant faded away, leaving nothing but his words thundering in Sarah's ears. It frightened her to feel tears stinging her eyes.

"We'll talk more about it," he said. "Later."

There won't be a later, Alex. There is only now. Tonight.

She looked up at him, putting on a bright, social smile. "And what about you? Where did you go after Cambridge?"

"Wow. Look what you've made."

He didn't know how much longer he could go on with the light talk, the studied charm, the empty social graces.

Alex examined the row of desserts on Sarah's kitchen counter and could only think of his desperate hunger for her. She'd tossed off her white jacket, and her silky black dress was driving him nuts. It had the little straps over her shoulders, just as he'd imagined, and it swirled around her body in a free, liquid way that set his pulse racing. Chocolate be damned. He wanted to devour *her* with his tongue, consume *her* with his desire. The effort not to touch her, not to get too close to the wall she'd built around herself, was exhausting.

He couldn't bear the thought of leaving her, either, not when he finally had her within his grasp, but that's what he had to do. And soon, before he made a fool of himself by throwing his arms around her and begging her to forgive him, or worse, tossing her on the bed and covering every inch of her nearly naked body with kisses. That would be an icebreaker, all right.

He'd promised himself to avoid anything personal on this important occasion, which he was determined would not be the last. He'd already broken his promise by asking her why she'd hidden away all these years, and making his first pathetic, futile attempt at apologizing. He dared not go any further.

He'd thought he would find her when the time was right and she'd come running back to him. What a stupid young fool he'd been.

"Crème brûlée," he managed to say. "You know it turns me into a slobbering madman."

"This is fudge pecan pie," she chattered on, her voice bright and brittle. "And, oh, this cake's a favorite of mine. The buttercream's fantastic. Taste." She dipped her fingertip in the zugertorte frosting and held it up to his lips.

He drew in a short, tight breath, watching the flush slowly climb her face as she realized what she'd done. It had been natural, he thought. She hadn't thought things through because she was nervous and uneasy, just as he was. What would she do if he took her finger into his mouth and swirled his tongue around it? She already anticipated it. He could see it in the softening of her mouth, the droop of her eyelids.

His body raged with an almost uncontrollable surge of desire as he physically felt a sensation he could not allow himself to experience even though she'd made the invitation herself. The air in the kitchen was still, hot, stifling, and time seemed suspended.

It was up to him. He had to maintain his tight control or lose her forever.

"Wonderful," he said, taking some of the frosting on his lips without touching her. He imagined he heard her let out a relieved breath, heard her heart begin to beat normally again.

"So would you like the cake, the pie or the crème brûlée?" Her voice seemed to come from a great distance.

"Yes," he said, enjoying her little laugh, even though it sounded forced. "Crème brûlée, of course, and a sliver of each of the others. No, a lot of each. Do you give out doggie bags around here?"

"BURLEIGH?" Alex said in answer to Sarah's question. "Has to be in his late sixties now. Never mentions retirement. Except for a few gray hairs, he hasn't changed a bit. Mother didn't speak to me for six months after I stole him away from her," Alex said, then polished off the last bite of crème brûlée.

Burleigh, who had been Eleanor Asquith's butler and father figure to young Alex, was the last of a dozen or so loosely related topics of conversation that had gotten them through dessert and coffee. Alex turned down her offer of brandy. She wondered if he felt the same way she did, that relaxing would be their undoing.

Desire stretched between them like a taut, heavy rope. If either tugged, the other would topple and this farce, this forced politeness, would be over. She knew he felt it, too; she knew him too well, knew he wanted her as much as she wanted him. She also knew lust was all he felt, and realized she was beginning to wonder if it really mattered that he felt nothing deeper.

Of course it mattered. She would not, could not give in to her weakness. Alex's innate integrity was making it possible for her to remain strong.

"Well. This was just great. Thanks. It's late," he added abruptly. "I'd better go."

"Yes, I suppose..."

He got up from the sofa and she followed suit. "It's been a great evening altogether, Sarah," he said. Did she imagine the tightness in his smile, the tension in his throat as he uttered this banality? "Good to catch up."

"Thanks for thinking of my company. I have a fairly clear picture of what you want. The prospectus, I mean." Sarah fought to keep the words from sticking in her throat. "I'll have some concrete ideas for you in a couple of weeks."

His slight frown seemed studied. "Actually, I have to

be here next weekend. We can go over your preliminary ideas together.''

He was much too close to her. The air hummed between them, the song of hormones begging them to get even closer. ''Oh, but I can just fax, or send jpeg files...''

What she needed was not to see him, ever again. An e-mail relationship was just what the psychiatrist would order. It might be a good idea to consult one immediately.

''Yes. Of course. We'll see. So goodbye, Sarah. Thanks for remembering my sweet tooth.'' He gave her another tense smile, didn't touch her, and backed away toward the door.

The torture was almost over. All she had to do was smile back, open the door, let him leave, take two aspirin and retreat to her bed, alone, for twelve more years.

He opened the door himself, stepped through it, gave her one last glance from the hall, then made his way toward the elevator.

This was the perfect time to become speechless. Instead, she spoke out loud and clear.

''Alex.''

He turned.

''You aren't going to kiss me good-night?''

He took one step toward her. ''I wouldn't dare kiss you, Sarah.'' He hesitated for an instant, making some inner decision. ''First date, you know. Got to follow the rules.''

''But, Alex...''

God help her, because she couldn't help herself. His honest admission made the ache in her body more immediate, more demanding than the ache in her heart.

She wanted him so desperately she could barely remember the hurt, the anger, her vows of revenge.

It was her moment to hesitate, to make her own life-changing decision. Having made it, she held out her hand to pull him back into the room. "But it's not our first date, now is it?"

4

SARAH WAS TUGGING HIM into his own dream. He'd longed for it to happen, but it was the last thing he'd expected.

He'd figured their first few encounters—because there wouldn't be just one, he wouldn't allow it—to be tense and tortuous events that would require all the Asquith-Emerson charm and fortitude he could muster. Instead, Sarah's hand, a real hand, for this was no dream, was putting delicate but definite pressure on his forearm and sending a message no one could misinterpret.

"Come into my parlor," said the spider to the fly.

He desired her deeply, but he didn't trust her. He'd lost the right to her trust, thrown it away. It was possible she was simply increasing his pain, leading him on for the fun of pushing him away. The Sarah he'd once known wouldn't have done it, but this was a different Sarah, one who'd been hurt and was still angry after all these years.

The possibility wasn't enough to motivate him to resist her. The dream of making love with Sarah was more compelling than the fear of ultimate rejection, frustration, even humiliation. He followed her through the doorway and gently closed the door behind himself before putting his hands on her shoulders and lowering his mouth to her upturned face.

One touch of her lips told him she was scared, too, as uncertain as he was, and then he stopped thinking altogether. His arms slid swiftly around her, almost out of old habit, and as his hands found the fine, narrow bones of her shoulder blades, he devoured her with kisses, not even trying to hide the intensity of his need.

She responded like a woman who was dying for sex, desperate for it. Maybe that was all she wanted, but that didn't matter, either. He'd searched for her for years, and now he had her, right there in his arms. It wasn't the time to ask her if her intentions were honorable.

Or to tell her his were.

He tore his mouth away from hers. "Sarah." He could hardly breathe, much less speak. "If you're going to stop me, stop me now. Don't torture me." He buried his face in her neck, just beneath her ear, but couldn't stop kissing her, so he kissed her there.

He felt the shudder run through her. "I'm not going to stop you. I couldn't if I wanted to."

"Oh, Sarah." Relief geysered through him and he seized her mouth again with his. Her breasts pressed against his chest. He could feel the peaks of her nipples, and knew they were bare beneath the black dress. His hands slid down her back to grip her buttocks and mold her against him. She groaned, writhing in a tortuous rhythm as he slid the dress up and away, finding the narrow, lacy line of her panties.

"This dress is driving me crazy," he whispered, hearing the rasp of his voice as if it came from a great distance.

"I hoped it would." Even now, in the grip of a strong

emotion, he could hear the slight edge of amusement
that lay beneath her breathless words.

"When did you buy it?"

"Yesterday."

"You bought it to drive me crazy."

"Yes."

The very idea inflamed him, sent him nearly out of
control. She'd planned it, she wanted it, she wanted him
and was willing to admit it.

The conservative, proper and sensible side of him
said, *Wants me for what? And for how long?*

The wild man in him screamed, *Who the hell cares?
You've got her now, so take her.*

NOTHING MATTERED but the nearly incredible fact that
she was in his arms again. The years of resentment
melted away. She wanted him as much as ever. He
wanted her, had searched for her, was sorry for what
he'd done.

As he damned well should be.

Sarah waited for the familiar anger to return, but the
only sensation rushing through her was desire so hot it
was burning her alive.

The desperation, almost panic, she'd felt in him earlier
was gone, and the Alex she remembered was back, his
hands so assured as they stroked her, seduced her with
their suggestive rhythms. He had always thought of her
first, waited, held himself back until she was ready,
more than ready, begging for it. But she was a grown-up
now, no longer a shy schoolgirl. It was Alex who'd made
her a woman.

She guided him to the sofa, pushed him gently down

to it and straddled him, her dress slinking up until only her panties lay between the heavy, aching apex of her thighs and the hard ridge she could feel under his trousers. She rocked there, pushing his head to her breasts, remembering the way he'd always stroked her buttocks, just like that, just as he was doing now, until she was crazed with wanting.

A deep groan rose up from inside him. She could feel it, but it came out as a sigh, a rush of heat against her breasts, stiffening her nipples until they ached, too, as intensely as the rest of her.

He slipped the straps off her shoulders and another rasping sigh escaped him. His lips closed over her breast and for a moment, she stilled, concentrating on that one sensation, until the demands of the rest of her body made her move against him again. She was close to release even now, wet and wild with desire, needing nothing more than her memories and his proximity.

"I want to feel your skin against me." She could barely hear him. "I want to touch you all over."

"And let me touch you?" She breathed it into his ear.

"Yes." This time he couldn't disguise the groan.

She could hardly bear to lift herself away from him, but she did, holding out her hand, pulling him up, leading him to her bedroom.

His face was flushed, his hair tousled, plastered to his damp forehead. Heat radiated from him in the room that was already too warm in spite of the cool air from the ancient air conditioner, which did little else than make white noise in the silence. Facing him, she took the hem of her dress between her fingertips and slowly lifted it over her thighs, her hips, her stomach. It hurt as she tugged it over her breasts, so full and sensitive, until at last it was in the air above her head. She tossed it into a chair and reached out for his belt buckle.

His eyes were dark and dangerous in the dim light. His breath quickened. "I'll do it."

"No," she whispered. "I want to."

She did it leisurely, making him stand through the whole tortuous process, sensing that his legs were barely holding him up, feeling the shaking of her own as desire weighed her down. She slid his belt out of the loops, undid the fasteners at his waist, pulled the zipper down as slowly as she could bear, feeling the moist heat coming from him. Then left him there to unbutton his shirt, starting at the top, moving down his chest, letting her knuckles brush the crisp dark hair beneath. She felt his muscles contract with each touch, felt him hold his breath and expel it in a rush, hold, expel, until at last she reached the bottom buttons and it was his massive erection that throbbed beneath her fingertips. He sucked in his stomach. His arms moved instinctively to go around her, but she gently evaded him. She wasn't through with him yet.

She opened his shirt wide and he shrugged out of it. His impatience was obvious in his jerky, careless movements. This wasn't the cool, graceful, cultivated Alex the rest of the world knew. This was the Alex she desired, had never stopped desiring.

Years had passed. How many women had seen this Alex?

It wasn't a thought she could handle right now. Instead, she closed her hand around him, the hot, throbbing part of him, and could feel his patience come to an end.

Swiftly she slid his trousers and boxers—his ever-so-proper white boxer shorts, ironed, perhaps even starched—to his ankles. She closed her arms around him, pressed her breasts to his chest and whispered into his ear, feeling her breath come fast, hearing the words rasp. "I could just leave you like this, bound at the feet," she said, "and have my way with you."

"You're a devil," he whispered back. Barely letting go of her, he was out of his shoes and socks in an instant. He flung back the light summer spread that covered her bed, then slid out of his pants as he pressed her down against the cool sheets.

"Now it's my turn." His mouth suckled her nipple. His fingers gripped the elastic of her panties and slid beneath, tugging them down a little at a time, until at last his fingertips found the part of her that was hottest and throbbing most painfully. He halted there, stroking her with his thumb while his fingers slid inside her.

She writhed beneath his touch, driving him deeper, in a frenzy and coming now, hard and fast. Higher, higher, until suddenly she exploded inside. His mouth stifled her scream as she rode the waves, moisture covering her body, clinging to him as if he were a raft in a stormy sea. Her climax seemed to last forever.

Breathless, exhausted, she collapsed in his embrace, breathing hard, feeling nothing but heat—the heat of the room, of his body, of her own—and feeling more relaxed, more content than she had in...in years, she guessed. Twelve years? Maybe.

How could he have ended it?

She wouldn't think about that, couldn't think about it now. Instead, she snuggled into the curve of his body, feeling his tension as he waited for her to savor every second of enjoyment. "That was lovely," she murmured. "Thank you." Hearing his startled grunt, she rolled away. "So, maybe we can do this again sometime…"

On the word *sometime*, he caught her at the edge of the bed, imprisoned her between his legs, surrounded her with his arms, buried his mouth in her neck, cupped her breasts in his palms. His erection pressed hot and hard against her. "I know you're not serious," he growled. "You're a wicked vixen, but not that wicked."

"Want some cake?" she said breathlessly.

"And eat you, too?"

"No!" But the words thrummed in her ears, vibrated down her spine. "Well, maybe." She shifted against him, tilted her head against the sensation of his mouth beneath her ear and rolled back into the center of the bed with him. He covered her with his body, rested on his elbows and gazed at her for a moment. Her breath came faster. His mouth came down to hers slowly and stopped with their lips barely touching.

"Do you remember?" he said. "The first time? That night in the pool house?"

"Oh, yes." She threaded her fingers through his hair. It was thick, silky, satisfying in the way it teased her skin. "You'd been so patient, and I hadn't been teasing you, really I hadn't, I was just scared."

"I know. I didn't want to rush you. I wanted it to be perfect." His lips curved above hers. "I hoped you'd want to do it more than once."

"Well, it was perfect, and I did want—" *I do want*, she

thought, and, *I'll never be scared again, not after that night with you.* His mouth came down on hers, hot and insistent, as if the memory had proved too much for him. With a soft cry she moved beneath him and the kiss deepened with urgency.

They clung together, writhed together, skin against skin. He slipped his hands beneath her, balancing on his knees, being so careful not to crush her with his weight, and he was suddenly touching her everywhere, strumming all her chords. She wanted him so desperately that the pleasure of a few minutes before might have happened eons ago. She felt deprived, and knew what she was deprived of. The lower half of her body searched for him, urging him, sending him a strong message of her need to have him inside her.

An important thought distracted her for a second, and she struggled to cling to it. "Did you bring anything?"

He stopped everything he was doing, which wasn't what she had in mind, to give her a look. "Did I bring anything."

"Does that mean 'No I didn't bring anything,' or 'Of course I brought protection.'" She'd stocked up last weekend, when she thought she'd need them, but she wasn't going to admit it unless he wasn't prepared.

He rolled lazily over onto his side as if he weren't having the slightest problem with this untimely interruption. His body, his breathlessness, said otherwise. "I brought an arsenal. We Asquith-Emersons are always prepared."

"Oh, good," she said, trying to tug him over her again and failing utterly. "Where are they?"

"Everywhere. In my pants pockets, in my jacket pockets, in my shirt pockets. All I have to do is reach over the side of the bed...."

But he wasn't reaching over the side of the bed. Instead, he punctuated each phrase with a kiss to her throat, to each breast, to her rib cage, to her navel, which he explored briefly with his tongue before sliding his mouth down and down. She whimpered when his tongue flicked through the soft hair of her mound, then cried out when it found its mark.

"No! It's your turn."

"I know. And I'm taking it."

"Alex..." But then she was beyond speech, beyond reasoning, and could only feel the warmth of his mouth on her most private and sensitive spots, feel the caress of his hands. The sensations swelled inside her, flooding every cell with unthinking need until they pushed her over the edge into wave after wave of rapture and, at last, blessed release. For a moment she lay there trembling, still clutching his hair as he eased up beside her. When they were side by side, she circled him with her hands.

"Sarah..." It was a warning. Light came through the open door, showing her his heavy-lidded eyes, his flushed face and sweat-soaked body.

"Shh," she whispered, stroking him.

He groaned. "You're asking a lot."

"You're giving a lot."

"Not enough. It will never be enough." But at last he reached over her, blindly searching for that one last thing he had to do before they could be as close together as she wanted to be.

He slipped inside her so easily, as he always had, at

least after the first time, when he had been so careful, so slow, so tender. That first time. Her first time. Thinking about it raised the ache of desire building inside her to a higher plateau. Sensitive beyond his years, he had been with her. A caring boy. A caring man. He had so much locked inside himself that could only come out when he was like this, in the grip of an emotion that wiped out generations of Emerson reserve and caution. Locked in his embrace, feeling him at the edge of his control, she smiled into the dark and gave him everything she had.

He came into her with a strangled cry, and in his last desperate thrusts she joined him in a hard, deep spasm that feathered through her veins and out into her fingertips. For a moment she swam in the purest pleasure, the pleasure that only this man had ever been able to give her.

They lay quietly together, silent except for the rasping gasps of their breath. She tucked her head under his chin, her ear against a pulse that still raced. Without disturbing her, he spread his body out across the bed.

She stirred, stroked his chest. "You're hot."

"Was that a compliment or an observation?" His low murmur sounded amused.

"Both, now that I think of it." She yawned. "I'm sorry the air-conditioning isn't better."

"Is it on?"

"Afraid so. What did you think that sound was?"

"Garbage trucks."

"Too early for garbage trucks. That's the window unit."

He kissed her forehead. "I'm fine. You fine?"

"Better than fine." She paused for a moment. "Want some cake now?"

"Lots of carbs in cake."

"You need carbs when you're exercising."

"I need carbs."

She slid her rubbery legs over the side of the bed and sat there, waiting for strength to stand. "Wine?"

"Water. A gallon jug if you've got one handy."

She turned on the bedside light. The romantic concoction of eyelet, floral linens and lacy pillows that covered her bed was largely on the floor, looking as if it had been picked up in a tornado and spat out again. She looked at Alex. He looked about the same way, but he gave her a slow, sexy smile.

"What about a cool shower first?" he said. "Water, shower, cake."

"And then?"

He did a double take, but recovered. "We'll hold hands?"

"Hmm. Okay," she said. "It's a plan. Not a totally satisfactory plan, but a plan. I'll get the water."

"I'll get it." He rolled out on the other side of the bed.

"Then I'll change the sheets."

"Too much trouble."

"Burleigh would have them changed."

Alex turned back to take in the full impact of the war zone. "You're right. He would. But..."

"Get the water," she commanded. "For me, too. With tons of ice."

He caught the sidelong glance she gave him. He'd always teased her about her American passion for ice. Troublemaker. She was trying to start a fight. Well, she wasn't getting one out of him, because this was one of those moments when ice sounded pretty good. He'd like to lie down in a tub of it and maybe not ever get up.

Never getting up wouldn't be possible with Sarah around. He was already coming alive again. He slid into his boxer shorts and padded into her kitchen.

God, how he hoped he could keep Sarah around. Tonight had been nothing short of a miracle. He was still pinching himself. All he had to do now was not blow it.

Why was he so sure Sarah was the woman he wanted, had to have? Why had he always been so sure? What if she'd changed in ways he couldn't perceive yet? Her increased self-assurance was obvious, but he liked that about her. What if she had new habits that he wouldn't like?

He frowned. He'd never slept with a woman who changed the sheets in midepisode. At least he hoped they were just in midepisode, because he already wanted her again, and after that, he knew he'd want her again and again.

Fidgeting uncomfortably, he concentrated on his need for water and drank three glasses from the tap before he allowed another thought to cross his mind. His thirst somewhat slaked, the thought returned at once. He didn't want to get too deeply into the relationship until he knew he was here to stay. He didn't want to hurt her again.

Face it. He didn't want to give her a chance to hurt him the way he'd hurt her.

Ice. He found it in old-fashioned trays in the freezer. She had stacks of them. He popped out a bowlful of cubes, filled a pitcher with water and grabbed two tall glasses. On his way out of the kitchen he remembered that in the real world, nobody was going to come along and make more ice. He put everything down and re-filled the trays, carefully sliding them into the bottom of a stack. Every now and then he realized how spoiled he was, how much he had of everything—except love.

Burleigh loved him, would take a bullet for him, he suspected, and that was about it. He didn't think any of the women he hadn't loved had loved him, either. Wanted him, yes. Enjoyed the weekend trips on the pri-vate plane, who wouldn't? Lusted after his money, a few of them. But he hadn't broken any hearts when he said goodbye, which he invariably did after one date, one weekend, giving them one final dinner to be polite and a huge bouquet of flowers. Long before he ran the risk of being taken home to meet the parents or even the risk of being counted on.

It all seemed so empty now.

He found Sarah plumping pillows in clean cases with ominous energy. Ominous, but promising. He put ice in a glass, filled it with water and handed it to her. She drank deeply from it.

"You brought a spoon for the ice."

"I couldn't find your ice tongs."

"Sheesh," she said. "Like I have ice tongs. Ever hear of fingers? Aren't we a little late for germ control?" But she was faking that disgusted tone and he knew it.

"Into the shower, woman," he commanded her.

"We're showering together?" Big blue eyes, wicked blue eyes, stared at him.

"Damn straight." He swept her up into his arms and

carried her into the bathroom. "City's in financial trouble, can't go wasting water."

"New York's in financial trouble? Omigosh, how bad? Should I..."

He put her down. "Hush," he said. He turned on the water and tested it gravely with his hand, then turned to her purposefully. The look in his eyes told her the promised carbohydrate overload would have to wait awhile.

MUCH LATER, they snuggled together against a massive stack of pillows, empty plates resting in their hands. "Wow," Alex said, "do you eat like this all the time?"

"In a word, no."

"You don't always have three desserts waiting in your kitchen?" He put his plate on the night table, then rolled to his side and gazed at her, waiting for her answer.

Sated, sleepy and relaxed, Sarah still noticed that it seemed to matter to Alex that she'd done something special for him. No one who hadn't met his mother Eleanor Asquith would be able to understand. "Not even one." But she had to be honest with him. "Desserts are the only thing I've learned to cook," she confessed. "I make one occasionally and take it to the office." Okay, she'd had an apple tatin waiting last weekend, but that kind of honesty was more cruel than honest.

"Lucky office."

"Hmm." He didn't need to know the ways in which her staff was less than lucky. "Let them eat cake" didn't fly in the twenty-first century.

"Your aunt Becki made desserts."

Sarah froze, but managed to answer him calmly. "Remember the crème brûlée?"

"Yours was just as good."

"You've forgotten hers."

"Some things you never forget." He was silent for a moment, and then he said, "I'm sorry I'll never see her again. Do you feel like telling me what happened to her?"

She didn't answer at once, but turned a cake crumb over and over with her fork, chewing on her bottom lip, and when she did speak, she tried to get it all out as fast as possible. "She—she found out she was very sick. I guess she didn't want to burden Todd with a long illness, or maybe she was afraid he'd leave her when she told him."

A low sound of shock and sympathy interrupted her flow of words, but only briefly. "He wouldn't have. I'm sure of it." Her eyes filled with tears. "But she chose to...speed up the process a little."

His arms circled her. "Oh, God, Sarah, I'm sorry."

"Let's not talk about it anymore," she said. "Tell me about your life in San Francisco."

He hugged her hard, but accepted the change of subject. "Okay, I have a house in Pacific Heights where Burleigh rules over a staff of..." He broke off. "Burleigh sent you his best regards."

She pushed back from him. "He said it that strongly? His *best* regards?"

"Those were his very words."

"Wow. He must have been beside himself with emotion."

"Practically babbling. He suggested I bring you out for a visit."

She'd been trying hard to act cheerful, to put Aunt

Becki's tragedy behind her so as not to spoil the mood, but the idea of visiting Alex in San Francisco shook her. "How nice," she murmured. "I'd love to sometime."

"What about next weekend?"

She was wide-awake now and remembering that the roses she'd been smelling had thorns. She'd been weak enough to invite him in, to accept his favors and to give her own, and the time had come to pay the piper.

Even pipers could wait. If they couldn't, they were undercapitalized. "I can't possibly come next weekend. My business..."

Which drew her to the crisis in her office. When there wasn't even enough money for salaries, it wasn't the time for her to take off for San Francisco. That could be her excuse, anyway. It wasn't the time to get that close to him, see him in his adult life, meet his friends, renew her friendship with Burleigh, be waited on by his staff. That was the real reason. "I can't," she said simply. "Another time."

He was silent for several minutes before he said, "Can we...when can we...do this again?"

Could she let it go at one last night with Alex, for old time's sake? It was an unbearable thought, but one she had to consider. "Maybe we can. Sometime. Can I think about it a little?"

"Of course. I understand."

That was one of several amazing things about him. He probably did understand. He understood she had never forgiven him. He understood that tonight she'd gotten carried away by pure physical attraction.

That attraction was weighing on her now, rising

above every other concern. "We have now," she said. "Can we just enjoy the moment?"

His voice was a murmur. "I can, and am." He kissed her forehead.

She sighed, stretched out against him and put her arms around him to draw him closer. "We were going to hold hands."

He stroked her back. "I know something more interesting I could do with my hands."

As his fingertips slipped around her, down her sides and across her stomach, she inhaled sharply. "Well," she said, feeling breathless, "two can play at that game."

LISTENING TO ALEX'S soft, even breathing—Alex would never snore—Sarah stared at the ceiling. It was early morning and she was exhausted, but sleep was out of the question. What could she have been thinking of to let him into her bed—she'd practically dragged him there—and furthermore, to let him spend the night?

She'd wanted him too much. Always had. Still did.

How could she still want a man who'd hurt her so deeply? She hadn't forgotten, hadn't forgiven. How could she justify to herself, to her own pride, what she'd done?

The answer came, and she accepted it reluctantly. Alex had appeared at a time when she needed a man's physical love. Why couldn't that man be Alex? When she no longer needed him, she'd let him go, just as he'd let her go all those years ago.

It was possible that the night meant no more to him than she was determined to let it mean to her. Maybe they'd see each other a few times and the magnetism would lose its force. But his pursuit of her seemed quite purposeful. He'd been looking for her. It sounded as if he was hoping to resume their relationship just where he'd left off.

That night came back to her in an angry rush, the night she'd waited in vain for him to come for her. If Alex wanted more than a few incredible nights of passion, she'd simply love him and leave him. She could do it with a clear conscience.

She turned to gaze at him, at his dark hair against the pillow, his lashes lying on his cheeks. *Love him and leave him.* Easier said than done.

5

ON MONDAY MORNING the temperature had reached eighty-five degrees by the time Sarah started out for her office, and the local weatherpersons were threatening a high of ninety plus. It wouldn't have made waves in the desert, but it was unseasonably warm for New York in the first week of June, and as the heat built up in the asphalt, concrete and steel that made up the city, by late afternoon it would have all the atmosphere of an oven.

On her way, she stuck her head into the shop where she usually picked up another cup of coffee and a cinnamon roll or some equally decadent breakfast, but the very thought of hot coffee and calories made her scurry out empty-handed.

In spite of that and the fact that she could feel her navy eyeliner melting down into the corners of her eyes and her hair frizzing into an unruly mop, Sarah entered her office with a light step and a big smile. "Good morning," she sang, flapping her arms to cool herself off.

Jeremy and Ray looked up, startled.

"Oh, Ray," Jeremy said, "as I live and breathe, it's happened."

"What's happened?"

"Let me put it this way," Jeremy said to Sarah. "Watching you has been like watching my sister get through PMS. First she's nervous, then she gets mean and nasty, then suddenly—bam!—she's like a cow chewing her cud. Except with most women the whole cycle takes a month. You've boiled it down to a week."

"You're just jealous," Sarah said.

"Of PMS, uh-uh. Of the direction your love life took this weekend, I don't know. I'd have to meet him first."

"Don't talk that way, Jer. It's not nice." Ray moved his gaze from Jeremy to Sarah. "We are very happy for you, Sarah."

"You can be happy for her," Jeremy said. He sounded peevish, and Sarah couldn't blame him. "I'm happy for *me*."

"As long as you're happy," Sarah replied. She watched them earnestly, wondering why they both looked so wide-eyed when she said, "Everyone should just be happy. It's all that really matters in life." Having delivered the sentiment that was uppermost in her mind, she remembered the second. "Rachel," she called out toward the reception desk, "can we make iced tea today?" Without waiting for an answer, she went into her office and closed the door.

She dropped her bag on the floor and went to the windows. They were already dirty again, but who cared? Sarah smiled through the panes at the sunny morning. It was going to be one of those legendary New York summers, debilitatingly hot and humid, the kind that made you feel as if someone had dropped a hot, wet towel over you. She sensed it in every pore of her body. But that didn't seem to matter, either.

Her business and her sex life, maybe even in reverse order, were the only things that mattered.

Once she'd determined to relish the present with Alex

and let the future decide itself, she'd been able to throw herself into enjoying the rest of the time he spent with her. They'd spent most of it in bed, eating take-out food and leftover desserts, cuddling, talking, making love. He hadn't mentioned next weekend again, but she knew, somehow, that he wasn't through talking about it.

Another thing she knew was that she was out of sheets. She whirled to her desk to write down "Pick up laundry" on her PalmPilot, and was startled to see the door pop open.

"I had to see for myself," Macon said.

"See what?" Just thinking about sheets had sent her into an arousingly graphic daydream Macon had interrupted.

"You. Calm."

"Oh. Well, here I am." She gave him a warm smile and slowly blinked her eyes.

"My gosh." He muttered, "I gotta try it sometime," and closed her door behind himself.

Rachel attacked her next. "Here's your iced tea," she said, plopping a frosted glass down on the desk. "Did we get his business?"

"Whose business."

Rachel put her hands on her hips. "Humph."

"Oh! His *business!*" She felt herself blushing. She'd had a similar conversation with Alex, in which he'd said, during one of the moments they were actually dressed and having a conversation, "How soon can you have some ideas drawn up for the ad agency?" and she'd replied, "Ideas for what?"

"Oh, yes, we discussed the various projects thoroughly and...actually..." She paused, feeling herself stumble slowly but inexorably toward reality. "I believe I told him we'd have a presentation ready for his ad agency two weeks from this Friday."

Rachel screeched. "Two weeks! And you're just sitting here?"

"I guess I should be giving it some thought, shouldn't I?" Sarah said languidly. "Ask Jeremy and Ray to come in, would you?"

What had she and Alex talked about before dinner Saturday night? It would come back to her in a minute, she was sure. Everything else about the weekend was coming back to her like cannonballs from a medieval trebuchet.

"GREAT GRAPHICS!" Alex said, "with an exclamation point. Here's the number. I don't know why you've never heard of them."

Russ Rogers, his account manager at Sweeney and Swain, huffed a little. "They're in New York, I suppose."

"Yes."

"If you're determined, Alex, I'll work with them, although I personally feel that we have just as many choices in San Francisco as they have in New York. DesignMe did a fabulous job on your last order."

"Flat," Alex said, shaking his head. "The message went flat. Give Great Graphics! a try. I want something cutting edge."

"Alex, cutting edge is not what you want in a financial prospectus."

"Why not?"

"Your investors are old-money. The DesignMe job

was jazzy enough to knock them out of their spats and bloomers."

"Great Graphics! will strip them naked," Alex said. "This isn't a suggestion, Russ, it's..."

"I'll call."

"Send them a deposit." He named a sum that made the sophisticated, world-weary Russ gasp. "I'll get a check couriered to you today."

"That's a lot of money up front," Russ sputtered. "Are you absolutely sure this is what you want to do?"

"Never been surer of anything in my life," Alex answered breezily. "FedEx the check, okay? Get on it right now and ask for same-day delivery. A bank check. So she...so Great Graphics! can have immediate access to it."

"I heard that," Russ said.

"What."

"She."

"You imagined it. Send the check."

Russ delivered himself of a deep sigh. "It's your money."

"Money well spent. Trust me on this. And Russ..."

"What?" It came out like a whine.

"If this turns out well, I'll tell Jack you found Great Graphics!"

Jack Middleton was the head honcho of Sweeney and Swain, and not only was Alex's account with the ad agency decently large, he also served on the board of the opera, Middleton's obsessive extracurricular interest, and made a hefty annual contribution. "Okay," Russ whispered. "The check's in the mail."

"Not the mail," Alex reminded him.

"Figure of speech," Russ said. "FedEx, same-day delivery." He paused. "I will have to wait until the bank opens." After another moment of silence, he said, "I'd better wire the money."

Alex glanced at his watch. It was only eight in the morning. That's why he'd caught Russ at home. Hell, he was at work. Everybody else should be, too.

As soon as he hung up the phone Alex punched another button. "Carol?" he said quietly.

She was at his door at once, notepad, still her preferred method for remembering things, in hand. Big change from last week. Everything in his life had changed this weekend.

"Air-conditioning," he said, leaning back in his chair and steepling his fingertips. "I've gotten interested in air-conditioning. Assume you live in an older apartment in a city known for its hot summers...."

"I LIKE THAT IDEA, Jeremy. Run with it. See what kind of theme you can come up with. Ray..."

Sarah's desk phone lit up and the buzzer sounded. "Do you know a crazy lady named Maude?" Rachel said.

"Maude. She's not a crazy lady, she's a writer. She lives in my building. Put her on. Maude? Something wrong?"

"Two hunks are here with three big white things they claim are air conditioners," Maude screeched. "They want to go up and fiddle with your windows, install stuff. Whaddya want me to do. Honest to God, I'd give my whole net worth to live somewhere besides the first floor of this building!"

"I can't imagine what they're doing," Sarah said. "I didn't order any—" She halted. "Did they show you an invoice? Does it have somebody's name on it?"

She waited through a lot of grumbling, a brief shouting match with the two hunks, and a couple of despondent barks from Broderick. At last Maude came back to the phone. "Somebody called Emerson Enterprises ordered these babies," Maude snarled.

"Good grief," Sarah said. She ran a hand through her damp hair. "Emerson. That's who gave you the flowers Saturday night. Alex Emerson."

"Oh. Really?" Maude's voice was marginally less harsh.

"Give them a key, I guess," Sarah said, "and send them up. I can't imagine where they're going to put three. That kitchen window won't..." She halted. Two in the bedroom? Surely he hadn't been that overheated. Or maybe he had. Her face flamed.

"He sent you flowers?" Annie had slipped into the room carrying contracts and checks to be signed, and wearing a dreamy expression.

"No, Annie, we're past the flowers-and-candy stage," Sarah said, feeling as if she were floating in a dream of her own. "This time he sent something much more personal. Air conditioners."

As full as it was, her office seemed too quiet until Rachel's unmistakable heavy tread sounded in the hallway and her steel-edged voice sliced into the silence. "Look what else he sent you." She flourished a fax.

Sarah gave it a single glance. It was from the bank, confirming a wire transfer to the Great Graphics! account. "You don't mean *he* sent me money. You mean the Zweig Company finally paid up."

"No. He. Alex Emerson."

Sarah felt the color drain from her face. "He sent me *money?*" She jumped up from her chair in a sudden fury. "Now that, *that* is going too far! Call the bank and..."

"It's from his ad agency," Rachel said in a dry tone. "It's a deposit for our work. Not payment for your favors."

Sarah sat down with a thud, her humiliation complete. "It was very thoughtful of him to send a deposit so promptly," she said stiffly.

"Better than thoughtful," Rachel said. "Look at the size of it."

Jeremy sniggered and Sarah gave him a hard look. Then she took a closer look at the fax. "Omigosh. Oh, my. Oh my oh my oh my. It's huge." She looked up at her little gathering, feeling stunned. "Nobody has to give up his salary this month. Or next month. Or any time in the foreseeable future."

"We're getting paid and Sarah's getting..."

"Jeremy! You know, Jeremy, you are clearly a case of arrested emotional development. Let's behave with at least a shred of dignity around here, okay?"

"That's so sweet of him," Annie said softly, although she had taken the fax from Rachel with a firm and purposeful hand and a lustful expression. "He must know we're right on the edge. There's no precedent for a deposit this large. I think he's just the..."

"Annie," Sarah said, almost snarling, "please act like an accountant. Accountants aren't supposed to be romantics. They're supposed to be humorless, practical, fishlike persons."

"Well," Jeremy said, his hand on his hip. "She's back to normal, anyway."

At her cry of rage, they fled. In actuality, they sauntered out, giving her glances—some teasing, some dreamy, some knowing—over their shoulders. Yes, she was back to normal. The satiated feeling was what had fled, leaving her hot and needy, wanting Alex more than ever.

The clincher came a few minutes later when Maude made a second call. Her voice was warm and gentle. It was such a change that Sarah considered calling 911. "That third air conditioner? It turned out it was..." her voice nearly broke with emotion "...for me. It sits on the floor and has a pipe that sticks through the window. It works. It actually works." She paused again, apparently to get herself under control. "I'm cool, Sarah. Broderick is cool. Even my computer is working faster." One last pause. "Who was that masked man?"

Alex was making friends with Maude. Bribing her. It meant he was coming back. Sarah's body warred with her mind. She wanted him to come back, couldn't wait for him to come back. But could she really give her body to Alex and keep her heart for herself?

Restless and flustered, she dug into her handbag for one of his cards. He'd left cards everywhere this weekend, she'd noticed. Being Alex, he had both business cards and personal cards engraved on rich cream stock. It was the business card she wanted now.

A warm, pleasant female voice put her through to Alex at once.

"Sarah, hello." The mere sound of his voice did such cataclysmic things to her body that she coiled in her chair to get through her little speech. "I called to say thank you," she told him. "For everything. For the air conditioners, for Maude's air conditioner, and especially for the deposit."

"Are the air conditioners cooling the place off?" His words were practical, but his voice was so sensuous that shimmery details of their hot night together came rushing back, as if they'd left her for even a second.

"I'm at the office. Maude says she's cool. More than cool. She's in a state of rapture."

"I'll have to see that to believe it."

"I expect you'll get a note and an autographed book."

"I'd rather see it."

Her heart thudded against her rib cage.

"And, of course, I want to check out those air conditioners personally before I pay the bill."

"I'm sure they're fine." Anticipation thrilled through her. "Don't worry about it."

"I want to see for myself how effective they are."

"I'll buy a thermometer on the way home."

His laugh was so low and rich that she was startled when he abruptly changed the subject. "Any exciting ideas for my promotional stuff?"

"We did a lot of brainstorming today." She distinctly recalled participating in the idea session. She just couldn't remember a word of it.

"I'll call you tonight. We can talk over your initial reactions."

She wasn't sure she could verbalize her initial reactions on the phone without getting arrested by the Fed-

eral Communications Commission. He must have a
high-tech telephone system, she thought uneasily. It was
almost as if he were there in the office with her, stroking
her with his voice. She had to pull herself together before her staff found her in a state of superheightened
arousal.

"I thought I'd be working directly with your ad
agency," she blurted out.

"I told you, I'm a hands-on manager."

She did not need to be reminded of Alex's hands. Feeling breathless, she squirmed a little in her chair. "Then
we'll all work together. Among us we'll come up with
something spectacular."

Something spectacular had already come up—her
feelings about Alex. Again she wondered if she could
protect her deepest emotions from his persuasive words,
his magical touch. It was essential. Only a fool would let
the same man destroy her a second time.

She said goodbye to Alex and hung up the phone, unable to concentrate on anything other than their conversation.

Voices intruded on her thoughts, as they so often did
in the casual atmosphere of Great Graphics! Ray and Jeremy were having a discussion in loud, excited tones.
"We think we've got it," Jeremy said, bursting through
the door.

"Hit me with it," Sarah said, smiling at them in spite
of herself.

"The youth market," Ray said triumphantly.

"This is a venture capital fund," Sarah said dubiously.
"Young people don't have any money."

Jeremy made an impatient gesture with one hand.

"I'm getting to that. We did some research on the Internet. Emerson Associates is only five years old, but it already has a reputation as an ultraconservative investment company."

"That certainly sounds like Alex," Sarah murmured.

"His capital comes from the old-money families of San Francisco. Don't get me wrong. He's aggressive. He works with billions of dollars."

"But," Ray said, raising an admonitory finger in the air, "there's a whole class of *nouveau riche* making billions in computer-related companies. He's missing out on all that money." He sounded reproachful, as though Alex had somehow been snobbish by not hitting up this younger group for venture capital.

Sarah had been able to drag her thoughts away from Alex's less conservative side long enough to get the point they were making. "Our designs," she said slowly, "could be his entrée into the new West Coast computer money."

"Right," Ray and Jeremy agreed, sounding like Tweedledum and Tweedledee.

Suddenly all business, Sarah leaned forward in her chair. "Give me some preliminary art ideas, Jeremy, and your notion of how the copy should read, Ray, and show me where you're going with this."

Four o'clock in the afternoon and she'd finally done some work. The weekend was over, she was past all that and was truly back to normal. Furthermore, she had money in the bank and brand-new air-conditioning. Let the summer be as hot as it liked. She would be fine.

AT TEN THAT NIGHT Sarah slid in between fresh sheets and balanced a novel on her knees. A glass of iced sparkling water sat on the night table beside her, and beside it, a hefty wedge of leftover cake. The room was as frosty-cool as a movie theater. What more could anyone ask out of life?

Just one thing, maybe. Feeling a little less peaceful, Sarah cut a large bite of cake and purposefully opened the book.

Next she adjusted the sleeves of her pink silk bed jacket, a nostalgic reminder of Aunt Becki, to whom it had originally belonged. For a moment the old sadness returned as she imagined her beautiful aunt waiting in her old-fashioned four-poster bed, wearing this jacket over a white silk gown while she waited for her lover, a man who might be able to break away and come to her or might not, who might be able to call her in private or might not.

Sarah would prefer lonely nights and occasional sex for the rest of her functional life to living like Aunt Becki had, and there was a strong possibility that was exactly what she was going to get. She gave the telephone a grim stare just as it rang, and made herself count two-and-a-half rings before she picked it up. If it was a telemarketer, he'd be sorry. He'd probably quit his job in tears after she got through with him.

"You weren't asleep, were you?"

She curled into the pillows, willing her pulse to slow down. "No. I'm just sitting here feeling cool."

"Where?"

"In bed."

"Ah. What are you wearing?"

"Alex, for heaven's sake. You sound like an obscene caller."

"This is *not* an obscene call. I was only wondering if the newly reduced temperature of your bedroom had driven you into your winter pj's."

His offended tone, coupled with the pure joy that rose inside her, made her want to tease him. "It has driven me into a bed jacket. Does that answer your question? Or would you like to know what I'm wearing under the bed jacket, if anything?"

"Sarah. Behave yourself."

At least he was loosening up. Maybe the thought of the bed jacket had done it. "It is deliciously cool in here," she said solemnly, "and I have you to thank for it."

"Your electric bill's going to go up," he warned her. "Would you consider letting me..."

"No. Enough is enough. Besides, today you made me a rich woman. Well, a solvent one, anyway. I thank you. My staff thanks you. Maude is considering dedicating her work in progress to you."

"Stop! I can't take any more thank-yous. Besides, there's no such thing as a free lunch. I expect a lot in return."

Sarah drew in a sharp breath. He couldn't mean what she thought he meant.

"Promotional materials that make an impression," he added.

She let out the breath. "Ray and Jeremy had a bright idea today. I don't know if I should tell you now or spring it on you after they've fleshed it out."

"Here's a compromise. I'll come to New York this weekend and they can tell me about it."

Sarah wriggled a little more deeply between the sheets, feeling the silk of her gown move against her breasts, moving across nipples that were stiff and aching. How she wanted his hands to cup them, his mouth to kiss them. But she had to retain some control over this situation. "We said a week from Friday. I think it would be better if you waited until then. And you don't need to come here. I'll send the materials to the ad agency on disk."

Was she crazy? Was she lying here in a state of arousal telling just the person she needed to take care of it not to come and take care of it?

He didn't react with the enthusiasm of a man whose real interest is in promotional materials, either. She was holding her breath again, hoping he'd argue with her at least.

"It's not the materials I want to see."

His honesty cut through her stubbornness as nothing else could have. "I know," she whispered. She felt hot and damp in spite of the quietly whirring air conditioners.

"Next weekend?"

Yes, yes, yes! "Weekend after next," she forced herself to say.

His deep sigh almost undid her. "You want time to think."

No! I want you now. This minute! "Yes."

"All right. I'll fly in on Friday."

"Okay."

"We'll talk between now and then."

"Okay."

"Are you all right, Sarah?"

His voice was so deep and gentle. Her hips lifted instinctively as if she were already taking him inside her. "Yes, Alex, I'm fine. I..." Should she say it? "I liked being with you. I enjoyed being with you. I want to be with you again. I'm just...scared."

"I know. And it's all my doing. We'll talk about it."

"When I see you."

"Yes."

She hung up feeling flustered, frustrated and strongly inclined to call him right back and tell him to take a red-eye at once. But she had done the right thing to put him off. She did need time to think. To recover from the impact of him. To strengthen herself against emotional involvement.

She turned off her bedside lamp, lay back in bed and remembered she was still wearing the bed jacket. She sat up and slowly tugged it off, so filled with memories, loving ones and painful ones, that her heart could hardly contain them.

There was one thing Aunt Becki did have. Love. She and her film producer had loved each other. Deeply. Honestly. The things they couldn't have, marriage, constant companionship, children, public recognition as his wife, mattered less to Aunt Becki than the romantic relationship she had with her lover.

Or that's how it had seemed at the time. But what it had boiled down to was that Aunt Becki never quite believed he loved her, because...

Because, of course, he hadn't given her that final, permanent assurance of marrying her. He had cared more about his wealth and position than about giving her that assurance.

Was that the scenario she could look forward to with Alex? Was that the one they'd already played out as teenagers?

Her jaw tightened. She was going to enjoy Alex as long as he was enjoyable. When it began to hurt, she'd get out. Unscathed.

Impatiently she sat up again and clicked the television remote, channel surfing until she found an old movie. It was *An Affair to Remember*.

"Shoot," she muttered, and flicked it off. Instead of counting sheep, she counted the days on her fingers. Eleven days. She felt sorry for herself for having to wait eleven days for Alex. She felt even sorrier for her staff.

6

"Carol!"

"What!"

Alex raised an eyebrow at his assistant's tone. She returned a look so quelling that he decided not to speak to her about her insolence. He had been a little snappish, he supposed. He'd been disappointed to get back to his office from a meeting and not find a message from Sarah in the pile of pink slips Carol had handed him or on his voice mail. "Who the hell is Elizabeth Winship?"

"A close friend of yours. Sir."

"A close friend of mine? No, she isn't. Never heard of her."

"She told me quite clearly she was an old friend."

"Winship." He thought a minute. "I know some Winships...Libby! Libby Winship! I'll be damned."

"Your accent, Alex. It's sliding back across the Atlantic. You asked me to call your attention to it on those occasions when you went all stuffy British on us."

"I don't recall saying 'all stuffy British.'" He glared at her.

"Perhaps not. The term may have been my own." Carol whirled on one heel to leave. Then she whirled back. "Are you sure you can't go to New York this weekend instead of next?"

"Absolutely." His mood darkened.

"I hope no one murders you between now and then."
This time she actually left.

He directed a snarl at her retreating back, but realized
she was well within her rights. Before he found Sarah
again, he'd been a stable individual who had his libido
under tight control. Sometimes he had a woman friend
who enjoyed casual sex and sometimes he didn't. He
acted like the same sensible, even-tempered, mannerly
person whether he was getting any or not. Sarah had his
mood swinging like the pendulum on Big Ben.

He glanced at the phone message again. It would
cheer him up to return Libby's call. How could it not?
Good old Libby. He could just see her, a freckled, red-
haired tomboy. He and his mother had spent many
weekends at the Winships' country estate, and they
were among the good memories of his childhood.

It was a London number on the pink slip. Too bad.
Would have been nice if she'd been in town, available
for lunch. Good old Libby, he thought again as he
punched in the number.

"Libby!" he said with enthusiasm after someone, a
housekeeper or a secretary, had put him through to her.
"It's Alex. What a surprise to hear from you."

"I wasn't sure you'd remember me." Her voice was
grown-up now, elegant but sweet.

"How could I forget? I'm not sure I ever saw you right
side up, though. You were usually hanging from a tree
limb."

"Was I ever that limber?" She sighed. "Let me assure
you I haven't hung from a tree limb in quite a while.
Wreaks havoc with the panty hose, y'know."

Alex laughed. "What's up?"

"I've decided I need to do something with my life."

"Ah." He couldn't imagine where this conversation was going.

"Unfortunately all I can do is speak languages. I wondered if you needed anyone in your office to handle international transactions."

This was a surprise. "What languages do you speak?"

"I'm proficient in oral and written French, Spanish, Italian, Portuguese and German. I'm conversational in Chinese and Japanese and I'm learning the characters, and I'm capable of ordering a meal in Eastern Europe."

"Sounds to me as if you've already been doing something with your life."

She sighed again. "Just traveling around. Visiting friends. Spending several months in this place or that. You can't shop and dine all the time. So I hired language instructors."

"Good for you. Let me think about this, Libby. Languages really haven't been a problem in this office. I may know somebody who could use your expertise, though." He really wanted to do something for Libby. She'd been a delightful teenager, and he appreciated that she didn't have much incentive to become a part of the workforce, given the Winship financial holdings. However, he'd like to encourage her not to waste her charm and her talents living the aimless life of an heiress.

"I don't want to be pushy," she said with some reluctance, "but I have to make a trip to New York soon. Do you have any plans to be on the east coast? We might get together there and talk."

Alex chewed on his lip for a second. He didn't want to

give up a second of his precious time with Sarah the weekend after next. Still, he and Libby went back a long way. Sarah would like Libby. They could all have dinner together.

"I'll call you back," he told Libby. "Give me an hour or two to see what I can set up."

He dialed Sarah at once. He'd called her on a dozen pretexts and now he actually had a reason. He gave himself a few minutes just to enjoy having her on the line, then got right down to business.

"Sure, I'd like to meet Libby," Sarah said, and it sounded as if she meant it.

Alex's eyes narrowed as another thought crossed his mind. She'd repeatedly mentioned a guy named Macon who worked for her, seemed very fond of him. He wanted to meet this Macon person a lot more than she wanted to meet Libby, and this was his best chance.

"A foursome would be more relaxing," he said. "Who could we ask to be Libby's date?"

"Well…"

"I know who," he said, before Sarah could actually come up with a candidate. "That guy in your office. Macon something."

She hesitated. "I don't know if that's the best idea." She lowered her voice. "Macon is, well, Macon is…"

"Attached to somebody else?"

"Oh, no," Sarah said.

"Gay?" Wouldn't that be wonderful.

"Absolutely not." When she laughed, Alex felt a rush of jealousy that surprised him. "He just wouldn't be my first choice to escort a British socialite to an uptown restaurant."

She didn't want him to meet Macon, and that confirmed his determination to meet him immediately. "Macon is a perfect choice," he said firmly. "You'd never guess Libby was a British socialite. She was always like one of the boys. Check it out with him. Tell him we're going to The Four Seasons. Call you later. I promised Libby I'd get back to her."

Perplexed, Sarah hung up her end of the phone. Why this obsession with having poor Macon escort a woman who was undoubtedly tall, lanky and long-faced, who'd talk through her nose about "Mummy" and "Daddy" and her "darling horses"? But Alex had asked for it and he was going to get it. She stood and went to her door.

"Macon, Ray, Jeremy, could I have a minute?"

The wary way they entered her office told her all she needed to know about the mood she'd been in while counting the days until she'd see Alex. She gave them a smile she hoped was a reassuring one and said, "Sit down. Coffee? Tea? Cola?"

"No, thanks."

"Uh-uh."

"Why?"

"Because, Jeremy," Sarah said, "I'm giving each of you a half day off this week." She smiled at their poker faces.

"Why?" Jeremy asked again.

"Because I have to ask you a tremendous favor."

"I knew it," Jeremy muttered.

"I need the two of you to come in for a while on Saturday afternoon to make your presentation to Alex."

"Goody, he's coming back!" Jeremy said. "That'll clear up the atmosphere around here."

Sarah made herself keep smiling.

"I guess we expected that, didn't we, Jer," Ray said. "We'll be here and we'll be impressive."

"Macon," Sarah went bravely on, "I want you to come to dinner with Alex and me at The Four Seasons Saturday night."

Macon blanched. "Aw, Sarah," he said in a plaintive tone. "Why?"

"That's Jeremy's line," Sarah said. "But I'll give you an answer. Because Alex is bringing a woman friend and we want you to be her date."

Macon's face broke out in perspiration. "Date," he rasped hoarsely. "Date? *Date?*"

"Don't think of it as a date," Sarah said. "You're making it a foursome."

"I have p-p-plans," Macon said at once, and mopped his forehead.

"I know," Sarah said kindly. "You'd planned to explore uncharted territories on the Internet. But instead you're going to have a fabulous dinner with three nice people. She's a childhood friend of Alex's. Apparently she's a down-to-earth lady who won't scare you."

"I'm not scared," Macon whispered.

"You're petrified," Jeremy suggested.

"Yeah. Petrified." He cowered.

"You'll be fine," Sarah said, not at all sure herself. "You do know you'll have to dress..." she moved her hands rapidly "...up."

"I can loan you a suit," Ray said. "It's a powder-blue..."

"Black," Sarah said. "Or dark blue. Can you, ah..." She knew he could afford to buy a suit if he didn't already have one hidden away for weddings and funerals. The thought of the suit he might pick out gave her chills, but Alex had been so oddly insistent that Macon should go with them.

"I guess Cleo would help me with that," Macon muttered.

Sarah felt greatly encouraged. Cleo was the owner of the town house on Perry Street where Macon occupied the fifth-floor eyrie. She was a dress designer, and if Sarah ever felt she could afford a designer original, she'd buy one of Cleo's. "Great," she said with a show of enthusiasm. "Put yourself in Cleo's hands. We'll pick you up." It was the only way to be sure he'd show up.

RAY AND JEREMY REHEARSED their presentation to the staff and received a standing ovation. Macon pronounced himself to be as ready to go out in public as he would ever be. Sarah had groomed herself to the teeth and had made a lemon tart, a hazelnut torte and in a fit of hominess, an old-fashioned chocolate cake with Seven-Minute Frosting. She also had a cold steak salad ready for dinner. It would be ten before Alex arrived from the west coast, and she had a feeling they would not be going out.

In fact, she knew they would not be going out. She wouldn't *allow* Alex to go out. She had no intention of letting anything stand between his arrival and tossing him into her bed. She knew that was what he wanted, too. It lay unspoken between them that he would come to her and stay.

Nothing was left to do but wait and wait for his arrival, and she felt she'd already waited as long as any human being should be asked to wait for anything short of a degree in medicine. With each passing minute her tension grew, along with an almost unbearable need to feel him locked tight inside her.

He stirred up her expectations with a call to say he'd left right on time in the company plane and was looking forward to seeing her. When the telephone rang at nine she almost made a dent in her ceiling. "There's a headwind." Alex sounded as glum as she felt. "I'm going to be at least thirty minutes late."

She put on a good act, she thought, murmuring words like *understandable* and *can't be helped.* She didn't do as well when he called at ten-thirty.

"We don't have clearance to land yet," he said. Now he was biting off his words. "Your president's making a departure or something of the sort. Add another thirty minutes. Oh, hell, I don't know how long this is going to take."

If she hadn't been so anxious to see him she might have been amused. "Your president," he'd said with a little added emphasis on the *your,* and his accent had definitely regressed. She'd always loved his native accent, had been sorry to see it become American and slangy. He wanted to fit in. She understood that. But it excited her to hear the clipped tones of the uptight British Alex and know his other side, his passionate, unrestrained side, so intimately. It did something to her insides. And he was making no attempt to hide his own frustration at the delay.

It didn't make the waiting any easier. Poised at the edge of the sofa as if he might walk in the door at any second, Sarah felt a growl rising from her throat.

Nervously she fiddled with the neckline of her white silk lounging pajamas. Trying to find something to wear that didn't say, "Here I am in my nightie, so make love to me," but also didn't say, "Here I am, all dressed up for a night on the town, so buck up and let's party," had stressed her ingenuity to its limits. Why was she so obsessed with appearances, with what Alex would think?

With other men she was simply herself, making it clear what she wanted. With Alex, she was playing a game.

She got up and moved restlessly around the living room. It wasn't a game. She had to make a choice; cling to the anger and mistrust of men that had been the emotional heritage of loving Alex all those long years ago, or welcome back the one man with whom she apparently had at least a chance for lasting happiness.

She hadn't decided yet. Until she did, she mustn't let Alex know how she longed to see him, how impatiently she waited for his footsteps in the hall. It reminded her too much of the way Aunt Becki had lived, waiting for Todd to show up, and when he didn't, handling the disappointment as philosophically as she could. Sarah couldn't live that way, wouldn't accept that role, not ever. Its costs were too high.

At last she heard the sounds she had longed to hear—a car door slamming in the street, her door buzzer ringing, the creak and ping of the elevator, the footsteps. She flung open the door to see Alex himself, a bag in each hand, looking hot, rumpled and harassed. In two strides he was inside the room, exuding the energy of frustration and desire as he dropped the bags on the floor and took her in his arms. All at once there was no thought of choices, of appearances. There was only Alex, all muscle and heat, strength and tenderness, home in her arms at last.

They had no time for anything but each other. He made one concise, definitive comment on his experience, "Damned airplanes." After that there was no conversation but the murmurings of lovers, soft sometimes, or harsh with need, and the cries of release. Through the long night he gave her every pleasure a man could give a woman, raising her to the heights of purest sensation that drove everything else from her mind except sheer delight that the man she'd always wanted was in her bed and plundering her very soul.

At last they slept, curled together, still tense, still not quite willing to admit the night was over.

"DO YOU EVEN KNOW how to make coffee?" After expertly tipping coffee from the grinder into the filter cone, Sarah sent a glance in Alex's direction.

Bare-chested and barefooted, fresh from the shower, he examined the coffeepot with an analytical eye. "It looks self-explanatory," he said. "Coffee in here, water in there, switch on."

"So if you were stranded on a desert island, you could at least make coffee for yourself until someone came to rescue you."

"Wouldn't be quite as self-explanatory on a desert island," Alex said. "For one thing, I don't know how to make electricity. Come on. Get stranded with me. We'll make electricity together." Still drowsy, already aroused again, he put his hands on her narrow shoulders and massaged them, feeling the small bones, the silky skin under his touch.

"Are you sure you wouldn't rather have Burleigh stranded with you?"

He reflected on his options. "I don't think so. I'll know for sure after I taste your coffee."

She gave him a soft punch in the stomach and slipped out of his grasp to pour glasses of grapefruit juice and lay pastries on a plate. "Let's take this back to bed, lie around for a while, read the paper."

"When's the meeting at your office?"

"Two o'clock."

He wanted time for talking. There were a few things he had to say to her, important things that might make a change in the atmosphere, soften her brittleness. As charming as her feistiness was, he could feel the tension inside her when he was around, tension that would persist until she had a better idea where he was coming from and where he intended to go.

But he had to sneak it up on her. She had a clever way of deflecting conversation she didn't want to engage in.

She could have been a diplomat. The most smart-mouthed, undiplomatic diplomat in the corps, to be sure, but a cagey negotiator.

"Look, a corporate tax cut," Sarah said, glancing at the front page of the Saturday *Times* as soon as they were settled back in bed.

"Burleigh said to say hello," he started, doing a little deflecting of his own.

She glanced up. "Not as passionate a greeting as last time. What have I done to offend him?"

He smiled at her. "Burleigh was always crazy about you."

"He was crazy about *you*."

"Thank God."

"Crazy enough to leave your mother in the lurch."

"'My own son,' she said, 'stealing my servants.'" Alex shook his head.

Sarah's eyes narrowed. "That was an uncanny impression you just did." She stared at him a moment longer, the paper lying limp and neglected in her hands. She hesitated. "How close are you to your mother these days?"

"I send extravagant bouquets on holidays. She makes a point of telling me where she'll be on holidays so she won't come home to dead flowers."

"Seriously," Sarah said.

That was supposed to be his line. If Sarah wanted the truth, she must really care about his answer. "Seriously, she no longer has any control over my life." He was on the right track, but now that the conversation was under way, he felt enormous pressure to say everything just right. He glanced at Sarah. Her eyelashes, pale and free of makeup, fluttered above her downcast eyes.

"I suppose she didn't ask you to say hello to me or give me her best regards."

"I haven't had an opportunity to tell her we've seen each other again. We don't talk about our personal lives."

Sarah scooped a lavish quantity of butter onto a bit of croissant and added a glob of strawberry jam, then began to thumb through the newspaper with her left hand. "Here's the front section," she said after a moment, giving it to him before picking up *Arts and Leisure* for herself.

Alex sipped coffee and tried to take an interest in the war news. Beside him, Sarah snuggled close.

It felt good having her lean against him like that, so good that he resented it when she moved away. It couldn't have been anything he said. She hadn't given him a chance to say anything. His eyes wandered to the newspaper page she'd been reading, and there was his answer.

Eleanor Asquith, star of...

He skipped the credits, but before he could make it to the next paragraph, Sarah's gaze darted toward him and she folded the paper. "You don't want to read about it," she said.

He felt tight all over. "No, I don't want to, but I'm going to." He took the paper from her hands.

...heads for the divorce courts again in a bitter fight with husband, Landon Reade, following her all too public affair with...

Sarah gazed at him as he read. He didn't want to know what was in her eyes, or in her thoughts. When she spoke, though, her voice was gentle.

"I guess you and she don't have to talk about her personal life. Hers is in the paper."

The old bitterness and embarrassment welled up in him. "I swear she marries these guys just for the publicity of divorcing them."

"Well, then, best reason not to get married." She no longer sounded quite as gentle. She moved even farther away from him. "Don't worry about it. It's her life. She's having fun. These are good croissants, don't you think?

Oh, dear, look at what happened to the stock market this week."

He bit his lip to hide his frustration. Even six thousand miles away, his mother had the power to affect his life, humiliate him, freshen Sarah's anger.

"Check the bond market," he said, giving up hope for a serious conversation. "I think the news is better there."

"WELL," ALEX SAID a few hours later. "Well, well." He stared at the computer printouts in front of him. Then he gazed thoughtfully at the two men who'd just presented the craziest, most pop-culture proposal he'd ever sat still for. His was not a pop-culture-type firm.

Not that he was going to tell the ad agency to cancel the contract and scrap the deposit. If he hated the stuff, he just wouldn't send it out. Mike would be impatient with him about the wasted money, but he'd cover the sum from his personal account. As long as it didn't affect Emerson Associates, what did it matter?

The wary way Sarah watched him told him he'd better not say he was appalled by the idea of sending out this garish trash under his firm's name. Stuffy Alex. That's what she'd think.

Okay, so he was stuffy. Better than being a public embarrassment like his mother.

"You're going to have to talk me into this," he said at last. He forced a smile. "Sarah will tell you I'm a throwback to a more..."

"Formal era?" Sarah asked sweetly.

He gave her a look. At least she hadn't said repressed. Or priggish. "You could say that. But I'm open to change." A muffled snort from Sarah made him send her another warning glance. "This is a new company, so maybe it will attract young investors. Give me your spiel one more time."

An hour later, he said as encouragingly as he could, "Continue in the direction you're going. I bet I'll be crazy about the finished product."

"You hated the brochure ideas," Sarah accused him on the way back to her apartment.

"No, I didn't. I just didn't understand them. The copy had a sort of rhythm. I don't know what to call it. Sort of da-da-da-da bop, da-da-da-da—"

"Rap," Sarah said with a look of scorn on her face.

"Rap. You really think a guy with a couple of million to invest will get the point?"

"I think a guy who's interested in putting the couple of million into a *music* corporation will. This particular company is a music company. What do you think they're recording? Opera?"

"I didn't ask," Alex said. "I just looked at the balance sheets, the price-earnings, the…"

"Bor-ing."

"Not if it's the business you happen to be in."

"Oh, okay, you have a point." Sarah sighed. "Just give me the word," she conceded, "and I'll send Ray and Jeremy back to the drawing board."

"No," he insisted, "I want to give this a chance. Worst that can happen if this promotion doesn't work is that I get you to do another prospectus, a little more traditional this time."

"Worst for you," she said cheerfully. "Sounds pretty good to me."

"How do you feel about cutting that chocolate cake when we get back?"

"Enthusiastic. Will you put frosting on my tummy and lick it off?"

"Sarah! Behave yourself."

But that was exactly what he would do. He could already taste her.

7

"AWESOME," ALEX SAID. His gaze roamed to the low vee of her neckline, to the slim lines and midcalf length of her simple black silk dress, to her black satin mules with the huge red roses on their pointed toes. Apparently mesmerized by the shoes, he took a step in her direction.

She backed away. "Don't you dare mess me up. I showered this morning, I had to shower before we could meet Jeremy and Ray and again before I dressed tonight. I'm going all pruny."

"You don't look pruny to me." He dragged his gaze upward as he took another step, and with one fingertip he traced her neckline, brushing the swell of her breasts. "Don't feel pruny, either. Wonder if your mouth feels pruny."

She neatly sidestepped his kiss, running away from the look in his eyes. "We have to leave right this second. I don't trust myself in a room alone with you. Besides," she looked up, dazzled by the very sight of him, "I can't wait to walk into a restaurant with a man who looks like he stepped out of a *GQ* ad." She stroked the perfectly tailored lapel of his dark suit. He'd packed his own clothes steamer, at least Burleigh had. His shoes had had cedar shoe trees in them. Here was a man from another world. "Savile Row?" she said.

"Off the rack at Nordstrom's," he said, sounding rather proud of it. "Burleigh found it."

"Burleigh buys your clothes?"

"Well, yes." He said it the way another man might say, "Well, yes, I brush my teeth regularly."

"Then you had it tailored, and now it looks like this."

"It did have to be tailored, yes."

"Did Burleigh go with you to the tailor?"

His Adam's apple moved up and down almost imperceptibly. "No. Wong Li does. Isn't it about time to go?" he said abruptly.

"I suppose we should leave a little early," she murmured, wondering who Wong Li was. "We may have to flush Macon out from under the bed."

"What do you mean, flush him out from under the bed?" Alex asked, after they'd braved the searing heat and crushing humidity of the summer night and were settled in the car he'd hired for the evening.

"Macon is...well, Macon's a classic computer nerd," Sarah admitted.

"Really?"

Sarah was surprised at how pleased he sounded. She'd been at the beginning of an apology, or at least a caveat. "Yes. I mean, he's so smart, I love him to death and couldn't function without him, but Macon is...terminally dorky. Socially challenged. A loose cannon on a quiet street."

She felt Alex relax beside her on the seat. "I'm *so* glad we asked him," he said in a satisfied voice.

"You think Libby will like a nerd?"

"I think I'll like a nerd."

She frowned. "I don't understand. Is he your date now instead of Libby's?"

"Okay, I'll confess. You mentioned this guy often enough to make me jealous. I wanted to meet him. This was my chance."

Sarah felt something close in on her. Alex was jealous. He cared enough to be jealous. It was an exciting thought, but also a scary one. His attitude toward their relationship was different from hers. Otherwise, he wouldn't care if she had a little thing for Macon. She certainly didn't care if he had other women waiting for him in San Francisco.

Other women. Nope, she wouldn't go there. Of course he had other women. How could he not? But she didn't care. She really didn't.

"That's very interesting," she said, giving him a reproving glare. "I wasn't jealous when you said we were taking Libby to dinner." Or had she been? She couldn't remember. She did remember making a point of sounding enthusiastic about having dinner with the dear old friend. But that was only because—

"You weren't jealous because there was no reason for you to be jealous. You'll see when you meet her." Alex smiled. "Good old Libby. Her parents' country house was a comfortable place to spend a weekend, and I haven't seen her since I came to the States with Mother."

If she'd felt any jealousy, which she surely hadn't, it had vanished. "If Libby is what you say she is, maybe they'll actually like each other," she said with a relieved sigh.

"I like him already."

"I hope you still like him a couple of hours from now."

"Why? Does he eat with his hands? Chew his own toenails at the table? Anything I ought to know about ahead of time?"

"Of course not. It's just that he doesn't always say exactly the right thing."

"A bit tactless, you mean. I'm sure Libby has a hide like an elephant's. Don't worry about it. Here we are." He paused. "Can that be Macon?"

Macon was, in fact, waiting for them in front of Number Seven Perry Street. He was probably waiting for a speeding taxi to jump in front of, but he was there.

And he looked unbelievably good. He looked so good that Sarah drew in a surprised gasp of air. She couldn't pinpoint all the changes Macon had wrought in himself, or more likely, Cleo Rose Hampton had wrought in him, but she could clearly see he wasn't wearing his Coke-bottle glasses. And his suit looked as good as Alex's.

The body inside the suit wasn't as good as Alex's, nor was the face above the suit, and nothing about him made her knees weak, made her heart lurch with anything but friendship, but no man could do that when Alex was around. Viewed objectively, Macon looked fantastic, like an entirely different man.

"That's Macon? The nerd?" Alex folded his arms across his chest.

"Doesn't he look great?" She couldn't hide her pride.

"I was going to sit in the front seat so you two could talk, but now I think he'd better sit in the front seat by his own damned self," Alex said.

"Alex, hush," Sarah said. "You don't understand. This is a transformation.

"Macon," she said, when he'd climbed in beside the driver and she'd made the most perfunctory of introductions, "you sure clean up good." She could tell from Alex's stiff posture that she'd used an American slang expression he hadn't heard before.

"Will I do?" Macon wriggled himself around in the seat belt until he was facing them. The expression on his face wasn't as confident as the cut of his jacket. "Cleo got really bossy. The contact lenses are new. I can only wear them two hours, then I go blind. Or put on my glasses."

"Put on your glasses," Alex growled.

"Oh, thanks," Macon said, sounding relieved. "So, Alex, how's life in San Francisco? Ever worry about earthquakes? Because one of those babies, if it's a big one, could mess up a guy's lifestyle, end it, even."

Each of Macon's attempts at conversation seemed to make Alex happier, and by the time they'd reached the restaurant, he'd relaxed completely. The Four Seasons was a large, elegant restaurant with lofty ceilings. He'd requested a table beside the reflecting pool, the location of choice. They'd been a few minutes early and Libby hadn't arrived yet, so he told the headwaiter to bring the fourth member of their party to the table, giving the man her name and a brief description.

While they waited, they ordered drinks. Macon asked for a rum and Coke and introduced the scintillating topic of fiber optics. Fortunately Alex had a certain interest in the subject since his firm was thinking of buying a company whose potential success depended on fiber optics. Sarah slowly sipped her Cosmopolitan and tried not to yawn openly. The evening was going swimmingly, except that the purpose of the evening hadn't been for Alex and Macon to bond, but to allow Alex to renew his acquaintance with Libby and to steer her toward possible employment.

They were still missing Libby.

Desperate for a break from fiber optics, Sarah opened her menu and glanced at the first course offerings. There weren't any prices on it.

The headwaiter approached their table, hovered uneasily for a moment, then said, "Sir, excuse me, but we have a person at the reception desk who insists she's the fourth member of your party."

Alex looked up. "Good. Bring her in."

"She, ah, her appearance doesn't, ah, is considerably different from the description you gave us. Sorry to disturb you, but we feel it would be best if you brought her in personally. Increased security, you know."

Alex growled deep in his throat.

"Want me to come with you?" Macon asked. "In case there's trouble?"

The look Alex gave him said, kindly but all too clearly, that in the event of trouble, Macon would be the last person he'd want riding shotgun. The look, of course, was lost on Macon, who slid his chair back and gave every impression of following through on his offer.

"Stay here and entertain Sarah," Alex ordered him. "I won't be a minute."

"You didn't give us the full picture," Macon said when Alex's back had vanished through the doors to the reception area of the restaurant. "You didn't tell us he was so, ah, totally virus-free."

She certainly hoped so! Startled, Sarah gazed at Macon's innocent face for a moment and then said, "I think you meant to say he's good to look at. Well, Macon, let me tell you here and now that looks aren't everything."

"He's pleasant enough, too, as far as I can tell."

"He's polite."

"What's the difference?"

"Pleasantness comes from within. Politeness can be taught, and is taught to privileged children who go to dancing school and especially to little English children who have professionally trained nannies."

She looked around for possible spies, then sneaked Alex's menu onto her lap. "Oh, my God," she said when she'd absorbed the general price range. Stunned, she slid the menu back onto the table. Dinner for four would cost five times what she'd paid for her dress.

She'd barely put the menu in place when Alex reappeared in the doorway. His expression fell somewhere between furious and stunned. Beside him a waiter bowed and babbled what were undoubtedly apologies. But all these images faded to the background when Sarah glimpsed the woman beside Alex.

Good old Libby did not, in fact, fit the description Alex had given the headwaiter. She was tall. Curly, flaming red hair haloed her face and fell below her shoulders. Her eyes were so green, their color was apparent at forty paces. But her physical appearance was only the first act of the drama.

She wore scarlet, a short, sleeveless, low-necked dress with matching shoes that sported gold stiletto heels. Her earrings dripped down to her shoulders, and the diamonds on her fingers sent dancing spotlights onto the walls. As this vision moved gracefully toward them, hips swaying gently, Sarah imagined a drum cadence, boom, ba-ba boom, ba-ba boom.

The incongruous touch was that Libby was blushing.

Only a few seconds had passed, but to Sarah it seemed like an endless triumphal march by the time they reached the table.

"I'm Elizabeth Winship," Libby said in a low voice, holding out her hand first to Sarah and then to Macon before Alex could even get his mouth open to introduce her, "and I'm humiliated."

HUMILIATED WAS NOT the right word to describe the way Alex felt at the moment. Embarrassed by the scene at the reception desk and the march through the restaurant with a hooker-type at his elbow, yes. Afraid of Sarah's suspicion and wrath, most definitely.

Libby had changed. She'd still be able to hang upside down, though. Her dress was so tight it wouldn't even slide. If you looked at her closely, at the skin of her breasts, which were practically leaping out of her neckline, you could see the faint freckling that was all that remained of her polka-dotted childhood appearance. He glanced at Sarah just in time to see her watching him looking at Libby's breasts.

He wished Macon would close his mouth.

Alex wished he could slide under the table and not come out.

"I'll never get used to American attitudes," Libby was saying, still blushing hotly, which was the only thing that made her seem remotely familiar, like the Libby of old. "You sound so slangy and casual, but when it comes right down to it, you are the ultimate Victorians."

"Puritans," Sarah murmured.

"Whatever," Libby said, sounding sulky.

Alex shot Sarah a glance. How mad was she? Wouldn't it be great if the situation had amused her instead? Her face was deadpan. He couldn't tell what was going on in the razor-sharp brain behind her beautiful face. Much more beautiful than Libby's face. And Sarah's dress was just as sexy as Libby's, but what Sarah gave off was an air of class. Class that was hers by nature, that hadn't come to her from breeding or training.

He was so focused on Sarah that he missed the signs of danger approaching. Macon had closed his mouth, which relieved Alex's fears that he might actually start drooling, but now he had opened it again. He gasped for oxygen once or twice and then said, "It's not the dress. It's the general impression."

Libby turned on him slowly. "What general impression?" The words dropped with the thunk of ice cubes hitting the bottom of a glass.

Alex found himself praying, which he didn't often do. *Please don't say it, please don't say it.*

"You look very glamorous, which wasn't the way Alex described you."

Now Libby turned on him. Her eyes shot shards of emerald into his. "How did you describe me?"

"He said you were tall, thin, freckled and tweedy."

There had to be classes Macon could take to cure his diseased conversational skills, a disease that would be terminal if Alex could get his hands around the man's throat. To his surprise, Libby laughed.

"Didn't your mother tell you I'd changed just the tiniest little bit?" She was still looking at him, but her eyes had softened to green pools.

What he felt wasn't Libby's warm gaze, but the tightening of Sarah's body, and next, the stroke of Libby's hand on his knee.

He froze. But only for a second. Then he countered by putting a caressing hand on Sarah's knee. He felt a sudden jolt.

Macon jumped. "What," he said.

Alex could only gather that Sarah had kicked Macon. All that remained was for Macon to put a hand on Libby's knee, which it was clear Macon was dying to do, but wouldn't dream of doing, and their warm little circle would be complete.

"Wine, yes," Alex said gratefully to the sommelier. "We'll start with a bottle of this," he pointed blindly toward the expensive end of the list of California whites. "And open a bottle of...of..." he shuffled the pages clumsily to the French burgundies and threw caution to the winds, "this to go with the main course. Bring the Chardonnay at once," he said, feeling desperate.

Libby had removed her hand. Maybe it had been nothing more than a friendly gesture, which would be good news. To his left, Sarah wasn't responding to his hand on her knee, which was bad news. "So," he said briskly to Libby while giving Sarah's knee a tentative squeeze, "you've seen Mother recently?" Sarah, he noticed glumly, leaned back in her chair and folded her arms across her chest.

"At Wimbledon," Libby said. "We had a nice little chat between sets. She encouraged me to do something with my gift for languages and said you were just the person to give me a start." Now her expression was hopeful. Alex began to think she hadn't changed that much after all.

"Do the three of you work together?" Libby said next, graciously including Sarah and Macon in the conversation.

"No," Sarah said.

"Yes," Alex said.

They stared into each other's eyes. Sarah's were glittering.

"I'm doing a design job for Alex," Sarah said with ominous politeness. "I work for him rather than with him."

"I work for Sarah," Macon chimed in. He was leaning toward Libby, resting his chin in one hand and gazing at her soulfully.

"Oh, I see," Libby said. "Are you two a couple, as well, or just professional colleagues?" She looked first at Sarah, then at Macon.

"I am completely unattached and available," Macon said.

"Sarah and I are the couple," Alex said smoothly. "We invited Macon to make it a foursome. Makes conversation easier, don't you think?"

"Are you free for brunch tomorrow morning?" Macon said.

The besotted man's tongue wasn't actually hanging out of his mouth; it just seemed that way to Alex. If Macon hadn't spoken, their table would have fallen into a deathly silence. Alex could tell his hair had fallen over his forehead, but for once he didn't mind, because under the hair he was sweating profusely. Still, he felt Sarah relax a little.

And sensed Libby's second humiliation of the evening. "I'm sorry," she said in a bright, social voice, ignoring Macon's invitation. "How gauche of me. Your mother didn't mention..."

"No," Alex interrupted. "I haven't talked to Mother recently." He felt bad about embarrassing Libby. Couldn't help it. "Was she at Wimbledon with her new beau?" he said, steering the conversation toward his own latest embarrassment. "The tennis champion? Ralph. Ralph something. I read in the paper this morning that she's divorcing Landon."

Libby sighed. "I don't think his name was Ralph," she said, "but yes, I'm afraid she was."

Alex's mouth set in a grim line. "I sense husband number six coming up."

"Madam," a waiter said, hovering over Sarah.

"The white asparagus to start and the sacrificial lamb," Sarah said. "I mean, the seared lamb tenderloins," she amended herself hastily.

"Excellent choices," the waiter murmured. "Madam?"

"The same," Libby said. Alex saw her lock her gaze with Sarah's. It was a look of feminine understanding. He didn't know what it meant. He wouldn't ask, either. He was afraid to.

"Sir?" The waiter leaned ingratiatingly toward Macon.

"The *fois gras*," Macon said, "and the tuna."

"The chef likes to serve the tuna rare. Will that suit?" the waiter said.

"Perfect," Macon said.

All eyes were on him now. Alex had expected Macon to ask where the hamburgers were on the menu and to order his well-done.

"Sir," the waiter said, and it was Alex's turn.

He hadn't had a second when he felt free enough from tension to look at the menu. "The, ah, bring me the *fois gras*, too, and the, ah, sweetbreads." He'd just ordered a dinner with more cholesterol than he'd had since—actually, just since he'd eaten his way through Sarah's collection of desserts. "If you'd like a soufflé, you should order it now," he instructed his guests. "I'll have the chocolate soufflé. Sarah? Libby?" *Heart, don't fail me now.*

He straightened his shoulders, firmed up his spine. *Perhaps you wonder why I called you together. To discuss Libby's career.* That was what they would discuss from here on out, and if he couldn't control something as simple as a dinner conversation, he wasn't a proper Asquith-Emerson.

"THANKS SO MUCH, Alex," Libby said sometime later. Standing on the sidewalk in front of the restaurant, she clutched the printed schedule of appointments he'd put together for her.

"Good luck," Sarah said. "And if none of these jobs suits you, I have some suggestions." She'd grown to like Libby. Libby wasn't to blame for the evening. Eleanor Asquith had engineered it.

"I'll get you a taxi," Alex said.

"No, no," Libby said. She pulled a cell phone from her tiny handbag and dialed a number. "I have my own car."

"About brunch tomorrow," Macon said.

He was back in his Coke-bottle glasses and Sarah's heart sank for him, ached for him when the moment came for this scarlet vision from another world, Alex's world, to rebuff him, a lowly computer nerd.

"Oh, yes," Libby said enthusiastically. "I'd love to have brunch with you. I'll pick you up at ten. Is that too early? What's your address? What I'd like most," she added, "is to go somewhere in the Village where we can sit outside and soak up this heavenly heat. Can you find us a spot in a place like that?" She gave him a dazzling smile.

"Bah, bah," Macon stammered. "Da. Wah. Here's my card," he said all in a rush, fumbling a card into her outstretched hand. "I'll make a reser...reser..."

If he fainted, could she catch him? Should she call 911 on the off chance that he was having a stroke? With his luck, he'd probably handed Libby his dry cleaner's card, or his stockbroker's.

"Here's my card, too," Sarah said, pressing one into Libby's hand. "If you need more ideas, or lose Macon..."

"Thanks," Libby answered. The smile she gave Sarah was both warm and faintly conspiratorial. "Oh, there he is," she said suddenly, turning toward a car that pulled up to the curb. "Bye," she said. "Dinner was divine, once I finally qualified for it." With a wave and a flash of red silk, slender knees and sparking diamonds, she vanished behind tinted glass.

Alex's car pulled in right behind hers, and he went toward it. "Macon," Sarah said, hurrying him along in Alex's wake, "where are you going to take her?"

"To Zanzibar," Macon said dreamily. Macon? Dreamy?

"Before that. Tomorrow. For brunch. Focus," Sarah hissed at him.

He gave her a magnified stare. "Les Deux Gamins," he said at last.

"Fine. Good choice. What are you going to wear? And for heaven's sake, talk about something *interesting*."

Before she could expand on this theme, Alex had ushered them into the car and they were on their way home. Her home. Where she would tell Alex—what?

The appearance of the new and improved Libby hadn't been his fault, either. But what was she to do about the insidious presence of Eleanor Asquith, who was in Alex's life whether he knew it or not, and always would be?

A deeper problem began to simmer inside her. What reason did she have to believe Alex wasn't just like his mother?

8

"SARAH, I'M SORRY."

"I know."

"I didn't. I mean, I didn't know that Libby..."

"I know."

"Sounds like Mother saw her and decided she'd be a good match for me. She set Libby up. She set me up. I didn't mean to set you and Macon up, but that's what happened."

"You handled it beautifully," Sarah said serenely, "as you always handle everything. You even said you were sorry, which isn't easy for men, I know. It was your mother's doing, as you said, and therein lies the problem. But can't we just forget it for tonight?"

They stood together in her living room. Of course, Alex wouldn't have said a word about the disastrous evening until they were in private. Too dangerous. She might make a scene, for heaven's sake.

He stared at her blankly. "Forget about it?"

"That would be my preference."

"You don't want to have a fight? Clear the air? Tell me how I took you out to dinner with a woman who flirted with me? Hit on me?"

"She did?" She could see from the expression on Alex's face that he wished he hadn't admitted the bit about Libby's hand on his knee, and this amused her, made her want to tease him. Sarah had noticed at once, could tell from the angle of Libby's arm. It was Alex who'd been offended by the evening. She was just...just finding it easier to keep Alex in the place she'd assigned to him—her lover for the long, hot summer ahead, a satisfied client, an expendable man just like all the other men who'd played cameo roles in her life.

Already she could feel her blood heating up for what she really wanted from Alex, all she wanted from Alex. She gave him a languid smile and laced her fingers together behind his nape, feeling the silken heft of his hair tease her skin, feeling his body tense up. "I can't fight when it's so cool in here," she said. "Earlier, on the sidewalk outside the restaurant in the heat, I might have been feeling a little scrappy, but not now." She moved closer, blew a kiss into his ear, pressed her breasts against his chest.

He groaned. "Sarah, what do you want?"

He meant something larger and more important, but she chose to interpret it her own way. "You know what I want, and you know just how to give it to me."

His voice hoarsened. He was giving up, giving in, going to play it her way. "What would you like first?" His arms slid around her waist and pulled her closer.

"Well," she said, pretending to think about it, "I really do think you should examine my entire body for skin damage due to excessive exposure to water."

"Pruniness."

"Exactly."

His fingertips went to the zipper that ran down the back of her dress and slid it down an inch. "I may have to ask you to disrobe to do a thorough examination."

"If you must," she sighed, moving sinuously against him, "you must."

His mouth moved across her cheek to her ear, where he nibbled at the lobe for a moment before sliding down to her throat. She shivered in the wake of his caress, warmth radiating between her thighs.

"You look pretty good so far."

"What a relief," she murmured, sagging against him. "Funny, I feel as if I could use a full-body lift."

"I don't think so." His voice vibrated against her collarbone. "Um, you're good here, too, and here—"

He slid the zipper lower, slipped her dress off her shoulders, flicked her skin with his tongue until it darted between her breasts. "Good, good... Aha. I found something pruny." His mouth closed over a stiffly puckered nipple.

Her back arched. "Therapy," she groaned. "It needs immediate therapy."

"Moisture," he mumbled, laving it gently.

"Heat," she whispered.

"You want heat, I'll give you heat."

"And pressure."

He lifted his head. His eyes were heavy-lidded, his mouth swollen. "Pressure?"

"The pressure of you against me. This...what you're doing...feels so good, but for heaven's sake," her fingers gripped his hair and her words came out in a moan "—can we get on with it?"

He laughed as he picked her up. "No. I'm not through with you yet."

He carried her into the bedroom, put her limp body down for a moment to throw back the spread. A host of lacy pillows cascaded to the floor. She didn't protest. Decor was the last thing on her mind. All she wanted was his skin against hers, his mouth on hers, him inside her, pounding, pounding.

She knew from the slow progress her zipper was making down her back that he was determined to make her wait for it. It was her turn to give up, give in, lie back and let him treat her to a night of the most delicious pleasure.

Sometime later he paused briefly in his tormenting, featherlight assault on the source of that pleasure. "Don't stop," she said breathlessly. "Don't..." She opened one eye. "Should I get a bikini wax or something?" Her voice was rough with arousal.

"Shh," he said, the sound whooshing into her, sending a stream of fire through her veins. "You're perfect."

Perfect. Perfectly happy, for this one minute in her life. Outside, a crew of motorcyclists revved up their engines in preparation for a race down her street. Her cry of ecstasy was lost in the tumultuous roar.

"LEAVING'S NOT AS MUCH FUN as getting here."

"Not for me, either."

Alex felt a cold wave of depression settling over him as he packed his bag, locating one shoe here, the other shoe there, mute reminders of the wild frenzy of their lovemaking the night before. Out of habit he put the shoe trees back in his loafers before he packed them, hung his suit neatly in its special compartment, put his soiled clothes in a bag designated for that purpose.

He was left with the two pairs of pajamas Burleigh had packed. If there was anything he hadn't needed this weekend, it was pajamas. Still, he wondered if it would be thoughtful of him to mess them up and add them to the dirty clothes.

"What are you thinking about?" Sarah had finished hosing down the kitchen after cooking an early dinner for him that had wrecked the place and employed every pan she owned. It had been a wonderful supper—a pork roast she'd marinated all weekend and roasted all day, acorn squash flavored with butter and maple syrup, a salad of red cabbage, apples and walnuts. A winter meal, she'd said, but as cool as the apartment was, why not?

She was waiting for him to answer. She seemed down, too, in spite of her efforts to sound sprightly, and while he was sorry, he took it as a good sign. "Pajamas," he said.

"No!"

"Yes. Whether I'd be embarrassed for Burleigh to find them unworn in my luggage."

"Oh. For a minute there I thought the honeymoon was over." She bit her lip and her face flushed hotly.

"I knew what you meant." He put his hands on her shoulders. They felt thin and tense. "The honeymoon will never be over."

"Alex..."

"Sarah, what are we doing here? What was this weekend all about?" He'd blurted it out, but now that he'd said it, he'd have to face the consequences.

"Sex." Her answer came too fast, sounded too quippy, and the red in her cheeks deepened. "We've been having sex. Not having a spell of amnesia, are you?"

"That's all it's about?" He refused to believe it, but her saying it hadn't surprised him. "Just sex?"

"*Just* sex? No. Spectacular sex. Mind-blowing sex."

"Not for me," he interrupted her, feeling his jaw clench.

"It wasn't all that great for you? Gosh, you could have fooled me."

"Sarah." She pulled away from him, turned her back to him, but he forged on. "I'm here because I love you. I've always loved you. I loved you then, when I was a kid, and I've never stopped."

She whirled, her face an unrecognizable mask of rage. "If you loved me so damned much, why did you leave me?" It was almost a scream of fury. "It was because of Aunt Becki, wasn't it? All these years I've assumed your mother engineered your vanishing act, but why should she care what Aunt Becki was? You're the one with the *dignity*." She hissed the word. "You had it even then. You just couldn't stand the thought of being hooked up with a woman with a seedy background."

"It wasn't Aunt Becki," he shouted back at her. "I loved her."

"Isn't that wonderful? You loved her. You loved me. So you decided a clean break was the way to free yourself from a person you loved who just wasn't in your class!"

"Class? What do you mean?" The idea outraged him.

"I was a virtually penniless orphan and the ward of a woman whose only source of income was her body. You were the heir to your father's fortune and a man bent on living a thoroughly middle-class life. I didn't fit your pretty little picture."

"That's ridiculous! If you'd shut up and let me explain..."

"Just tell me why! That's all I want to know!"

"Money!"

It stopped her in her tracks. She paled, stared at him, her eyes huge and brightened by the tears that welled up in them. "Money? Somebody *paid* you to break up with me?"

"Blackmailed me would be closer to the truth."

She could only stare at him.

His anger, which he knew to be anger at himself, drained out of him. He felt the tension flowing out along with it, felt the relief of finally cracking her brittle facade and getting his chance to talk to her about the only thing that mattered. He grabbed at that chance with both fists, no matter how painful, how final the conversation would be.

"You were right in the first place. It was my mother."

Sarah took in a breath through clenched teeth. "Your mother acts the way she does and had the nerve to disapprove of Aunt Becki?"

"No! Please, Sarah…"

"All right, tell me whatever it is you want to tell me." At the breaking point, Sarah was now a mere ghost of the woman who'd given him all her softness and warmth in the night. She stalked from the bedroom and sat down stiffly on the flowered sofa, imperiously directing him to a chair too far away from her to allow him to touch her.

He collapsed tiredly into the chair and expelled a deep sigh. "I don't know how Mother felt about your aunt. Mother's a sophisticated woman, if nothing else. I can't imagine she *disapproved*, as you put it. All I know is that she had a clear idea of the life she intended for me.

To her credit, she wanted me to have a proper education."

"Did you explain to her that I wanted the same thing? For you and me both?" Her lips tightened. "My idea of a proper education didn't require a Cambridge degree, but I wasn't pushing you to marry me."

"I told her. She told me she knew how long those lofty goals lasted when you were young and silly."

"She knew from personal experience."

"But she underestimated my willpower. And yours." If only he could cut through her time-hardened defenses, he could strip through the bitterness in her voice forever. "She said we'd end up penniless in married student housing having a baby a year. What she wanted for me was the life of a wealthy young gentleman. I could work if I wanted, not if I didn't, cruise the Mediterranean with a ship full of beautiful people, make the gossip columns, eventually pick out the flashiest of the women, marry her with lots of fanfare and spend the rest of my life being not so discreetly unfaithful to her."

"Just like Todd."

"Just like her." His own bitterness was surfacing now. "She was the trustee of the money I'd inherited from my father. She threatened to withhold it from me if I didn't go back to England with her. That very night, without seeing you, without even calling you. On top of that, she'd disown me."

Sarah's face was growing even paler. "You really did trade me for your money."

He couldn't stand it anymore. He stood up, circled the room. "It was more than the money. It was all I had of my father. It was my only source of independence from my mother. I told myself that once I'd come into my trust funds and didn't need her support any longer, I'd find you and make things right."

She was silent, but he could feel her fuming.

"And one more thing. She was, with all her faults, the only parent I had. I was eighteen years old. Can you let yourself imagine how it would feel to be eighteen and cast completely adrift?" At once he knew he'd said the wrong thing.

"I don't have to imagine," Sarah said in a low voice.

SHE'D BEEN FIFTEEN when she was cast completely adrift. But she'd had Aunt Becki, who gave her more love and attention than many kids got from their own parents, more love than she thought Alex had ever had in his life—until he met her.

She was furious with herself. She'd allowed herself to be dragged into this conversation, a conversation Alex had been trying to introduce from their first meeting, and she didn't want to go there. He would too easily be able to gain her forgiveness with his explanations, his obvious regrets. Her anger at him had been the driving force in her life for all these years. What would she be if she gave it up?

Anger had driven her to leave her high-school friends behind, take back her family name in order to hide from the past, to excel in college, to go from job offer to better job offer, always on the move until she felt financially secure enough to start her own business. Anger fueled her determination to make that business succeed.

All that fury, and all Alex was expecting her to say, was waiting for her to say, was "poor baby." He wanted her to take him in her arms and say she understood, offer him complete forgiveness.

But he wasn't a poor baby. He was a rich one.

It was true that he had been very young at the time he had to make his momentous decision. Momentous for her, anyway.

She was certain she would have made a different decision.

But then money had never played a big part in her life. Alex had explained that it meant something to him that went beyond the ability to have material goods. The money was his last connection with his father.

As these arguments, these rationalizations spun through her mind, she knew they were the reasons she hadn't wanted to give Alex his moment to speak. She knew she'd find it too easy to listen, because Alex was charming and persuasive, but also because she...

The end of that thought was too frightening to contemplate. Because she wanted him, that was it, and that was all. Even now, fighting mad, she felt the stirrings of desire, the heat creeping through her veins, the dampness between her thighs. But she'd only had two weekends with him. The thrill still wasn't gone. Eventually she'd have enough of him, her temporary needs would have been met and she could leave him without a qualm. Impatiently she shifted her position, all too aware that Alex waited for her to say something, anything.

Of course, she'd waited twelve years for him to explain himself.

That wasn't quite fair. She'd hidden herself away so

there wouldn't be the slightest possibility of his ever explaining himself.

She told herself sharply to cut it out.

"I can't take this in all of a sudden," she said bluntly. "I have to think about it."

She should have told him goodbye right then and there. She knew it as soon as he came over to her and knelt in front of her on the sofa.

"Can we still be together while you're thinking?" He said it gently, hesitantly, with none of the smugness of a winner.

"Yes," she whispered. An ache in the back of her throat told her she was close to tears.

"May I come back next weekend? Stay here with you?"

She was so filled with longing there was only one answer she could bear to give him. "Yes."

"I'll give you anything you want, as long as you want, except one thing. I can't share you with anybody else."

As if she could stand the thought of making love with anybody else. "I can't share you, either," she said, thinking of Aunt Becki. Her lip trembled. "Apart from discouraging Libby, are there any women you need to tell goodbye?"

"No. I did that already, right after I ran into you."

She was increasingly certain she was going to hurt him deeply when she ended their affair, but she steeled herself, reminding herself of her own crushing pain. "Have there been lots of women?"

His eyes shifted away from her. "Yes," he said reluctantly. Then his gaze met hers straight on. "Have there been a lot of men?"

"Some. Not a lot." Only when her physical needs overcame her reluctance to give herself to anyone.

"Have you ever been in love? I mean, since—"

"No." It was too great an admission. "I've been focusing on my career, getting my business going." She couldn't stop herself, although she knew the answer he'd give her. "Have you?"

"No. I don't think I've hurt anybody, either. I made my feelings pretty clear."

As he was making his feelings clear to her.

She couldn't take having his eyes on her any longer. She stood, went over to the bouquet he'd bought at a sidewalk stand and fingered the petals of the vibrant, salmon-colored gerbera daisies. "Next weekend," she said. "No pressure, okay? No soul talks. No—"

"Just sex," Alex said.

"Yes."

"As long as you want it that way."

"Your pilot must think you've been abducted."

It was a dismissal, and he recognized it. He got up slowly. "I'm on my way."

"Will you sleep on the plane?"

His mouth quirked up at one corner. "Like an exhausted tomcat."

"I packed up the rest of the carrot cake and the gingersnaps."

His arms went around her so tightly she could hardly breathe. "Thank you," he murmured into her hair. Then he lifted it off her neck and deposited a long, lingering kiss on her nape. "Bye."

She watched him from her window as he got into the

limo whose driver had waited patiently for almost an hour.

Goodbye, Alex. I— No, I don't love you! I don't, I don't. I won't.

9

"TO DI-I-I-E FOR."

"You tart."

"Ray knows he's first in my heart, but I had an urge to jump that man, I admit it."

"Ohh, why couldn't we have been here?"

"You mustn't flirt with the clients. I know Sarah made that very clear when she hired you."

"Maybe we ought to start thinking about..."

This was the jumble of conversation Sarah heard as she stepped down the hallway from the elevator to her office. It broke off in midsentence when she walked in to find her staff gathered around Rachel's desk.

"I've got a spreadsheet to balance," Annie said brightly.

"We'd better get to work, Jer," Ray said. "We've got a big job here."

"Yes, indeedy we do," Jeremy said. "I need help, Macon. My color is simply putrid."

While Sarah, filled with suspicion, gazed silently at them, they quietly flowed into their various cubicles. Annie clicked computer keys, shining with efficiency. Rachel picked up the telephone with a purposeful air. Macon frowned deeply as he made adjustments to the color capabilities of Jeremy's computer. Ray and Jeremy hunkered around Ray's monitor, a vision of busyness.

"Good morning," she said, folding her arms across her chest.

"Good morning, Sarah," they chorused.

She felt thrown off balance. "Well. If nobody needs me for anything, I guess I'll just..."

They all just smiled, except Rachel, who said, "Tea or coffee?"

"Coffee. Please." She stalked into her office. As soon as she closed the door behind herself, she smiled. They'd been talking about Alex.

Her telephone buzzed at once. "Alex on the phone," Rachel said.

Sarah picked up the receiver slowly, cuddling it in her palms. "Good morning," she said.

"I didn't wake up in time to call you at home. How are you?"

Wasted. "I'm fine. How about you?"

"I slept on the plane. I'm ready to roll."

"You made quite an impression on Ray and Jeremy and Macon," she said.

"I hope I impressed Ray and Jeremy with my interest in a prospectus that doesn't make my clients think they're being invited to a concert."

"Grumpy, grumpy," she teased him. "In fact, Jeremy has a crush on you."

"Oh, for God's sake."

"I scratched his eyes out with my fingernails."

"Sarah! Be serious. Does Jeremy understand I don't...I'm not..."

She was enjoying herself. "I don't know. Want to have a heart-to-heart with him?"

"No! He won't make a pass at me, will he? Because if there's the slightest possibility he might..."

"It's totally against office policy," Sarah said sternly. "Any such activity should be reported to me at once."

He was silent for a moment, and then he said, "It's a good thing you didn't have brothers and sisters. You would have tormented them until they developed serious psychological problems."

"Are you developing a psychological problem?"

"The problem I'm developing isn't a psychological one."

Shivers of heat traveled insidiously through her veins. She didn't need memories of her weekend with Alex today. She had work to do, important work, work that could save her business. But the memories came anyway, all in a rush, making her limp and needy. "Is there anything I can do to help?" she said softly.

"You have the only cure."

"We'll begin therapy on Friday. It will be lengthy," she said, "and will require a great deal of patience and cooperation on your part."

"Is it painful?"

"Only if you resist."

A low growl came through the line. "I'm tough. I'm up for any torture you can deal out."

"I'm sure you are. Even now, as we speak."

"You're evil, Sarah, evil, evil. I've got so much to do today, and how am I going to get interested in it now?"

"I was just asking myself the same thing." She sighed. "We are two debauched souls."

"Derailed."

"Demented."

"But having a good time?"

She felt he'd started to say, "But happy?" "Yes," she whispered to him. "Having a wonderful time."

SHE DIVED INTO HER WORK, distracted always by Alex's spirit that seemed to be hanging around in her office. The work going on, though, seemed, if anything, to increase in productivity. They saw several projects to completion, sold several others, and Ray and Jeremy were putting their hearts and souls into designing brochures for Alex's business that would not only make him happy, but get the positive attention of his ad agency, as well.

Hot and bothered with anticipation, on Wednesday evening Sarah began her preparations for Alex's arrival Friday night. The grocery store, where she bought staples, seemed unusually cold. Thoughtful of them, she supposed, but they'd overdone the generosity. She was shivering in her long black skirt and tank top as she started home with the heavy bags of flour and sugar, butter and cream, dishwasher detergent and sparkling water. A moment later, the piercing rays of the sun in the western sky pinned her to the steaming sidewalks, and she was dripping perspiration as she dumped the bags into the elevator.

But the heat was no problem this summer, not with her two new air conditioners. She turned them up at once, but the apartment didn't seem to cool down. Oppressed by the feeling that she was burning up, she took a cool shower. It had a dramatic effect. When she stepped out of the stall, she was freezing.

It wasn't possible, she simply couldn't accept it. She was getting sick.

She'd get up early in the morning and make the pie crust and the cookie dough then, and get some sleep. But she woke up the next morning with a painfully scratchy throat and a stuffed-up nose.

It wasn't fair.

She lay in bed for a while staring up at the ceiling, tears welling up in her eyes as she contemplated her immediate future. She had to call her office at nine when Rachel would arrive, and then she had to call Alex and tell him not to come this weekend.

Or maybe the other way around. But it was only 4:00 a.m. on the west coast. If she called him at 4:00 a.m., he'd think she was dying.

She struggled dizzily out of bed, went to the kitchen and made a cup of tea with half a lemon squeezed into it. One sip convinced her that her throat couldn't handle tea with lemon. Abjectly miserable, she forced herself to stay awake until nine, called Rachel, then drifted off to sleep. The telephone woke her up.

"Sarah? I'm sorry. You were sleeping."

"No, no," she lied, noticing that her body was already so hot she didn't even heat up at the sound of Alex's voice.

"I called your office. Rachel said you were sick."

He sounded upset. She struggled to sit up against the pillows and tried not to sound like a plague victim. "I was going to call you at some reasonable hour," she said. The clock said noon. "Like right about now."

"You sound terrible."

"Not as terrible as I feel. Oh, Alex..."

"I'm still spending the weekend with you."

"You can't come," she said miserably. "I look awful, I feel awful, I can't cook. You'll catch it from me. I'll give you a rain check."

"Nope." He sounded mulish.

She raised her voice. It hurt, but she did it anyway. "Do you hear me, Alex? You are un-in-vi-ted. Pretend to be reading my lips."

"I'm not coming to see you. I'm sending Burleigh to get you."

"Wait a minute..."

"I'd come myself, but I'm tied up until tomorrow. Burleigh will be there—" he muttered time lapses to himself "—by six at the latest."

"I don't feel like going anywhere," she wailed. "I don't feel like dressing. Just let me die here alone. It's better that way." With a loud snuffle, she pressed the telephone into the pillows and laid her ear on it.

Now he'd gone all soothing. Nurse Alex taking charge. "You don't have to do a thing. Just sleep until Burleigh gets there. Take aspirin. Drink juice. Watch old movies. You can sleep on the plane, too. I'll be sure Burleigh has some antihistamines with him."

"You can't force me to get on a plane and come to California."

"Of course I can't. That's why I'm sending Burleigh. I'll see you tonight."

"Alex! Listen to me!"

"You like orange juice better, or grapefruit?"

Her roar of rage had an excruciating effect on her throat. She deeply regretted having wasted it on a dial tone.

DRIFTING IN AND OUT of sleep, she realized that in addition to the sore throat and running nose, now she had a buzzing in her ears.

Damned virus. She drifted off again, but woke up when the buzzing turned into a ringing. That was the telephone. She'd know it anywhere.

"Sarah!" It was Maude, and she was shrieking.

"What's wrong?" Sarah croaked.

"I think I've got him!" Maude trumpeted. "The Village Voyeur. I caught him looking at my front window and I grabbed him."

"That's nice," Sarah said. "Well, thank you for..."

"Don't hang up! I can't hold him much longer. Call 911." The sounds of a scuffle followed, and after that, voices.

"The jig is up," Maude said. "He's got a partner. Oh my God, Sarah, he says he's coming after you!"

"Madam—" Sarah heard someone say.

"Oh," Sarah said dreamily, "that's Burleigh."

"He's burly all right," Maude said. "One of them is anyway. The other one looks like a damned actor."

Alex had meant what he said. He'd sent Burleigh to pick her up. Burleigh was a sensible man. He'd take one look at her in her rumpled, sweaty plaid flannel pajamas and know she was in no shape to travel.

If Maude didn't disable him first. "It's okay, Maude. Let them come up," she said.

"Are you crazy?"

"No, I'm sick. Burleigh works for the air-conditioner man," she explained. "Not the burly one, the other one. I don't know who the burly one is, but if Burleigh says he's okay, he's okay." The words *air-conditioner man* were the only credentials Maude needed to identify Alex.

A silence followed, an unusually long one for Maude, before she said, "It's out of my hands. If you're looking to get abducted, it's none of my business. But I'm coming up, too."

"I'll be delighted to see you," Sarah murmured.

Could she even make it to the door to let them in? She didn't have to; Maude used a master key. All of them marched into Sarah's bedroom: Burleigh, a tall, comforting presence flanked by an expressionless, muscular younger man, Maude and Broderick, who took one look at Sarah and bayed at an imaginary moon.

"Miss Sarah," Burleigh said, advancing toward the bed. "It's such a pleasure to see you again."

He wasn't wearing the uniform she'd grown accustomed to, but a tweed jacket. His hair had grayed a little, but otherwise he was the man she remembered, the man who'd been the closest thing Alex had to a father. "It's wonderful to see you, too," Sarah said sincerely, "but as you see, this is a very impractical idea Alex has..."

"Will you put your neck through here, Miss Sarah?" He was holding out an attractive caftan in summery blue-and-white stripes. "And your arm in here, yes, that's the ticket. Good girl. Here we go."

She was obeying him without thinking. He didn't seem the least bit impressed by her tangled hair, her unwashed face...good grief, had she even brushed her teeth today? Nor did he listen to her perfectly logical refusal to do something as silly as get on a plane and go to California.

"Rafe?" Burleigh said next, with a lift of one eyebrow.

The muscled young man reached into the bed, picked Sarah up in one smooth move and deposited her in a wheelchair he'd unfolded when he arrived.

"No, really," Sarah said. "This isn't at all the right thing..."

"Want me to shoot 'em?" Maude said.

It almost took more energy than Sarah could muster, but she managed to swivel her head toward Maude. She was holding an object that looked awfully like a pistol. It couldn't be, of course, and if it was, it couldn't be loaded, but still, Maude did write crime stories...

"No! Don't shoot," she said hoarsely, and immediately collapsed into a coughing fit. "These are the good guys," she choked out between hacks.

"You're sure?" Maude lowered her weapon.

At this moment, Burleigh chose to bend down and scratch Broderick between the ears. "Splendid dog, Madam," he said gravely. Maude lowered her weapon.

Personally, Sarah had given up the fight several minutes ago. At this point, she'd go with aliens if she could just close her eyes again.

Rafe wheeled her into the elevator, and at the ground floor, picked up the entire package, Sarah and wheelchair, and carried it to the curb, then put her into the waiting limousine. While he and Burleigh exchanged a few words, Maude stuck her head through the window. "Last chance," she said.

"It's really okay."

Maude hesitated again. "If it's really okay, is it okay to eat the chocolates they brought me?"

"Pig out," Sarah said, collapsing against the upholstery. "You're safe. Maude?" Her neighbor came back to the window. "Would you call my office?" she said. "Tell Rachel...tell her Alex will take care of me."

She barely recorded the trip to the airport in Westchester with Burleigh, where two pilots carried her into a small, luxurious jet and tucked her into an actual bunklike bed, where a man—could he be a real doctor?—examined her, took her temperature, and after questioning her briefly, gave her aspirin and antihistamine. Burleigh stuck with her like a Band-Aid, hovering unobtrusively, asking if she were hungry, thirsty, in need of the facilities—his words—until he sat down opposite her, buckled himself in, and the plane took off.

It was too much to get her mind around. All she knew was that she was safe.

She slept again. When Burleigh woke her to say they'd be landing in thirty minutes, she asked if there might be toothpaste on the plane. He produced a complete toiletries kit and helped her into the bathroom. She washed up as well as she could and brushed her teeth and hair, then slithered out of the flannel pajamas.

"Ditch these somewhere," she said, ready to collapse again.

"Yes, Miss." He was unable to disguise the sound of relief in his ordinarily toneless voice.

Her last memories before the world faded around her involved pulling up in front of a large, imposing house on a quiet, steep street. She vaguely remembered Alex rushing to the Mercedes in which they'd traveled from the airport, his picking her up in his arms and carrying her through the cool, dark night to a large, lovely room filled with fresh flowers. He slipped a soft white cotton nightgown over her head and tucked her between even softer sheets, held a glass of water to her lips, stroked her forehead, then kissed it. She managed to put her arms around his neck for the briefest of moments before they began to feel like lead and she sank back onto yielding down pillows, knowing with even greater certainty that she was safe.

WHEN HE WAS FINALLY SURE Sarah was asleep, Alex went downstairs to the kitchen in search of a cold beer. He was exhausted. He found Burleigh, who'd flown six thousand miles that day to abduct an unwilling princess, wiping glasses at the sink and looking fresh as a daisy in his customary butler's uniform.

Alex frowned. He wasn't sure Burleigh ever slept. He'd never seen the man eat or drink anything. He wasn't sure he was human.

"Have a beer," he offered, slumping down at the kitchen table.

"Thank you, sir," Burleigh said, "but I'll postpone that pleasure for a small nightcap later."

Ha! He drank. "What do you think?" Alex asked him next. There was no need to explain what he meant.

"Miss Sarah seems much the same as always," Burleigh said.

Alex peered around him, thinking he might have seen a slight change in the angle of Burleigh's jaw, as if he had smiled. "The face of an angel and the tongue of a serpent?"

"I wouldn't put it precisely that way, sir."

"But you wouldn't contradict me if I put it that way."

"I would never contradict you, Master Alex. I might add to your statement that the serpent under consideration would be a small garden snake who hisses only to warn you not to step on it."

Alex felt startled. It was hardly the first substantive statement Burleigh had ever uttered. Alex's youth had been shaped by similar statements, rare, but always wise. He'd been surprised every time.

He also recalled that his mother had sent Burleigh to England to ready the Surrey house for their arrival before she'd sat him down for the little mother-and-son talk that had changed his life, had almost destroyed it forever. If Burleigh had been there, could he have altered the course of events?

Alex sighed. Too late for that now. But not too late to win Sarah back. It couldn't be. "You would approve," he said carefully, "if Sarah and I..."

"Oh, my, yes, sir." Burleigh spoke the words in a flat tone.

Alex smiled, feeling laughter welling up in him. For Burleigh, that statement had been a passionate one.

"I'll do my best," he promised.

"And you shall prevail, sir. I'm certain of it."

Damn right he'd prevail.

10

FRIDAY AND SATURDAY passed for Sarah in a haze of antihistamine-and-illness-induced drowsiness. Between naps, she drank the chicken soup Alex brought her, ate tiny bites of ice cream and fresh fruit, listened to the compact discs he played or watched movies, the sillier the better, on satellite or DVD. As far as she knew, Alex was with her almost every minute of it, holding her hand or lying beside her with her head pillowed on his arm.

He took her temperature, gave her medicine, stroked her face with damp washcloths and rubbed her back. He talked to her in a low, quiet voice about soothing things—books, movies, plays they ought to see in New York, offbeat restaurants he'd read about. He brought a giant bouquet of fresh flowers to the room each morning.

Twice a day a small, elegant woman in a housekeeper's uniform came in, helped her into the shower, changed her sheets and towels, brought her fresh, soft cotton nightgowns and didn't leave until she'd settled Sarah back into bed. She always left a tray of tempting drinks and pastries and ushered Alex back in as she left.

Sarah made a firm decision that each time she caught a virus, she'd check into a small, expensive hotel to recover. Or she'd just come to stay with Alex again. Just as firmly, she put that thought away.

Late Saturday afternoon after her shower, she declared herself to be well, or close enough to it.

"Don't rush it," Alex warned her.

"I haven't," Sarah said. "I've hibernated like a groundhog for two days." She held out her hand and gave him a little smile. "It's been a lovely weekend. Too bad I can't remember much of it. What I'd like to do now is get up, put on something or other and walk around a bit. See your house and garden. Watch the sun set on the coast it actually sets on. Over. Whatever." She frowned. "I don't have any clothes, do I?"

Alex went to the closet, pulled out an extremely pretty lounging outfit and presented it with the flourish of a salesperson in a clothing store. "Will this do? Burleigh brought a couple of pairs of your own shoes."

"It's beautiful." It was pale lilac silk with a tunic top and loose, wide-legged trousers. "Where did it come from?"

"I picked it out myself."

"Well, thanks," she said, giving him an admiring look. "You did a great job." She hesitated. "Did Burleigh bring my own underwear?"

"Ah, no. I visited the lingerie department at Nordstrom."

"You naughty boy. What did you buy?"

He held up lilac-lace bikini panties and a matching bra, a bemused expression on his face.

"Aren't you clever? How did you decide on a size? Run around the department fondling the undies until the size felt familiar?"

"Sounds like fun, but no. I conscripted a salesperson, told her I wanted a half-dozen white cotton nightgowns, and then I pulled a corner of the tunic out of the bag and said, 'Do you have any unmentionables in this color?'"

"What did she say?"

"She said, 'We have the color, but we don't carry your size. You might try the Amazon Department on Five.' So I started over."

Sarah giggled, feeling better and more energetic every minute.

He paused, looking reflective. "Her face didn't change expression anytime during the conversation. If she'd waggled her eyebrows at me I might have been embarrassed. So," he said, starting to look more energetic himself, "I guess you'd better try everything on for size."

"You'll have to make the final decision," Sarah said, and waggled *her* eyebrows.

"Delighted to," he murmured, not embarrassed at all.

She slid out of bed, steadying her legs, which were wobbly from inactivity. Slowly she lifted the soft cotton nightgown over her head and heard him take in a harsh breath. "The panties first," she told him.

He lifted first one of her feet and then the other as she stepped into the panties, and she felt her body waking up to his touch, felt giddy with warmth and pleasure as he slid the bit of lace up her legs. He slipped his arms around her, caressing her buttocks while he brushed kisses across her cheeks and down her throat and pressed her tormentingly against his own aroused body.

"These seem to fit fine," she breathed. "Try the bra."

He drew away reluctantly, but his eyes lit up with

wickedness as he picked up the bra and held it in position in front of her breasts, slowly moving it toward her. He brushed the lace against her, and she shivered, leaning into the cups of the bra. With a featherlight touch he moved the straps over her shoulders, then put his arms around her to fasten it.

"I wanted a front hook," he said between the kisses he nuzzled into her hair. "They didn't have one in this color."

"Color is everything," she whispered into his throat. "You know, when the hooks are in the back, you have to sort of settle yourself into the bra to be sure it fits."

"Really," he growled. His hands slid back across her ribs, then reached into the bra to cup her breasts. "Like this."

"Um, yes, exactly like that, and then you push them up...oh, yes, like that, and..."

Her words were lost in his sudden embrace, his fiery kiss. He stopped himself long enough to say, "We can't do this. You've been very sick. You should be resting." He gently disengaged himself from her.

She gazed at him. "I do need to blow my nose," she admitted. She blew it vigorously, threw away the tissue and eyed him purposefully. "Come back here," she said, gripping him with all the strength she had and fitting herself against his body.

He groaned, but he obeyed. After all, she was his guest, and Alex had always been the perfect host.

"IT'S A MAGICAL PLACE. I can see why you love living here." At last, Sarah was seeing his house, his well-tended gardens in the light of an enormous moon that hung over the bay like the friendly face in children's books of fairy tales. They sat on a stone balcony sipping coffee after a delicious dinner produced by Alex's cook—Dungeness crab, duck in a sauce flavored with pomegranate molasses, a fresh cherry clafoutis served warm from the oven. She had been ravenous, which had delighted Wong Li.

"The Wongs are a lovely couple," she said.

"They're great. Wong Li drives me, too, and supervises the gardening. Wong Mai takes care of the house. Burleigh runs it all. Including me."

"With the quiet tenacity of a bulldog," Sarah guessed, remembering how neatly he'd managed her abduction. "Gosh, this is a great way to live." She leaned back contentedly in the lounge chair, wondering what it would be like never to have to think about doing the dishes.

Alex cleared his throat pointedly. "Notice the weather."

"How can I? There isn't any."

"That's the whole idea."

"Are you casting aspersions on the climate in New York?"

"Yes."

She sighed. "I can't blame you. It is nice to sit outside and still feel cool. Hard to believe it's almost July." She gave him a sharp sidelong glance. "How did you arrange not to have any fog?"

"With a large political contribution."

"You do have your ways, don't you?"

He looked smug. "Yes."

She laid a hand on his arm, filled with gratitude and feeling soft and warm. "Thanks, Alex. I would have been miserable this weekend all alone snuffling into my pillow and drinking bouillon made from cubes. Instead—'' She paused, wondering if she should be this open. "I've never felt as cared for in my life."

"I want to take care of you for the rest of your life." His voice was low. He didn't look at her.

"How can you possibly know that?" She didn't look at him, either, and moved her hand back to the arm of the deck chair.

"Sometimes you know."

"How long was your mother married to your father?" The air seemed to grow chillier.

"Four years. I'm not my mother."

She sighed. It had been wrong of her to say what she had after his kindness to her this weekend. "I know. I'm sorry. Sometimes I'm a little too direct for my own good or anybody else's."

"A grass snake, hissing a warning."

She could sense his gaze on her, and she turned to find him smiling. "Snake?" she said, curling her lip. "Now you're calling me a snake in the grass?"

"That was not the analogy I was making."

"I'm glad to hear it." She sniffed, which made her cough. Alex reached for a box of tissues he'd carried out to the balcony and held it in front of her.

"We'd better go in," he said gently. "You're still recuperating."

They rose, and Sarah drifted ahead of him into the magnificently proportioned, high-ceilinged Spanish-style living room of his Pacific Heights house. "You could put nine of my apartment in this room alone," she said, looking way, way up.

"Let's not," Alex suggested. "The moving costs alone would be staggering. We'll think of something else."

She gave him a little thump on the arm. "I should go home early tomorrow," she said. She hated thinking about it, much less saying it. "I need to get organized and go back to work on Monday."

"I'm flying back with you."

They started up the wide, curved staircase to the second floor. "You don't have to do that," she protested. "I'm fine. You don't have to send the plane, either. I can just..."

"It's all set up. Don't argue. I'll have to turn around and come right back, I'm afraid. I'm doing a takeover on Monday."

"Hostile or friendly?"

"Depends on how cooperative management is."

They reached the guest room. At the door, Sarah turned to him, stroked a hand down his cheek. "Would you like to stay with me tonight, germs and all?"

He bowed slightly. "The pleasure would be all mine."

"Not all," she said, and threw her arms around his neck as he picked her up and carried her into the room. "Oh, look, Alex. I do believe Wong Mai has changed the sheets *again*."

THEY ARGUED most of the way home. At least, Alex reflected, it distracted him from his constant desire to make love with her, which he could hardly do with the pilots popping in and out to smile and say soothing things about turbulence and headwinds in a southern American accent they must have learned in flight school.

"I'm telling you, Ray and Jeremy know what they're doing," she informed him. "So, actually, do I."

Her hair was a silky cloud of curls. Her eyes were giant sapphires, shooting sparks of fire. The air was thin up here in the stratosphere and he was turning into a poet.

"I'm willing to go with it if the agency approves it."

"The agency will love it, but they won't admit it if you don't take a positive attitude."

"Okay, I'll try to act positive."

"Just don't sound negative."

"Okay, okay." But he didn't really feel impatient. This was Sarah, and he loved her, admired her and enjoyed her energetic, contentious company. He felt as if he were waking up to a beautiful morning after a long sleep.

He wondered if the cabin pressure might have dropped.

Sarah had begun making notes and sketches on one of his office writing pads. Feeling restless, he unbuckled his seat belt and wandered around the cabin. "Want a candy bar?"

"What kind?"

One of the pilots had served them a tolerable lunch of sandwiches on sourdough rolls and salads from a catering firm. Otherwise, the plane was stocked with every imaginable junk food for the odd emergency or even whim. He opened the drawer in the galley and rattled off the list.

"I'll take a Snickers." She gave him a sunny smile, just as if she hadn't been challenging every statement he'd uttered since they got on the plane.

He hid his own smile. He was completely charmed by her, and he knew it.

He wondered if she did.

After he'd delivered the candy bar and a bottle of water to her, he examined his entertainment choices. He had DVDs, CDs, paperback books and a wide range of magazines. Alex perused the magazine rack, and his eyes lit up at the sight of last month's *Gentleman's Quarterly*. His pilot's idea of what Alex might like to read.

Normally that was a laughable idea, but today Alex needed something in the way of research materials. He had a problem he couldn't discuss with his tailor. How did you hide a persistent erection?

You dressed to the left or to the right and your suit trousers were measured accordingly, but no one ever mentioned dressing to the center. As a result, there wasn't much you could do when your abdomen size suddenly increased by several uncomfortable inches as his had now, just watching Sarah in action.

Women had it easy, comparatively speaking.

He picked up the magazine and read the table of contents. Not surprisingly, there wasn't an article that came directly to the point. So he'd look for clues in the photographs. Holding the magazine, he wandered back to the broad double seat he was sharing with Sarah.

Before he looked at the pictures, he decided to take a glance at the interview with a Fortune 500 friend of his, who'd done a great job of turning his little production company into an enormous production company. And he was a self-made man, he recalled, unlike himself, who'd had a pretty hefty head start.

He'd barely skimmed the first paragraph when Sarah said, "You're reading *GQ*."

Uh-oh. Her eyes sparkled with mischief. He was in for it. "There's an article here about..."

"Uh-huh. Sure. An article about knotting a tie to perfection."

"No, about a friend of mine."

"I just knew you were a *GQ* reader. But don't be embarrassed. I take *Vogue*." Her smile widened as she returned to her notes, and he knew she wasn't through with him. "Only for the articles, of course."

He huffed with annoyance. "I don't take *GQ*. It was in the rack, that's all. And I saw this article, so I..."

"What is your friend wearing?"

"What is he *wearing?* I didn't notice what he was wearing. I was reading about what he was *earning*."

"Oh, come on. Let's have a look." She took the magazine right out of his hands and turned to the full-page photo. "Armani. That's what he's wearing. The full Armani. Personally," she said, giving him an earnest, owlish look, "I prefer your look. I look at you and I don't think 'label.' I think good fabric, perfect fit. Oh, Alex, this is such fun, flying home in a private jet and talking fashion with you."

Damn her! But he couldn't help himself. He was laughing. "You asked for it," he said, and grabbed the magazine from her.

"His tie looks like Zegna," she said, still clinging to the page, "but everybody's doing a Zegna knockoff now, so you can't really be sure. And that's the whole point for somebody like him, right? For people to recognize the tie as a—"

He'd finally captured her mouth and rendered her speechless. "Now," he mumbled, "I'm going to tell you what I was really looking for in this magazine. I do have a fashion problem." He grabbed her hand and brought it to his hard, painfully throbbing groin. "You are skewing my measurements."

He heard her gasp, then felt her long, slender fingers surrounding him, stroking him through the light fabric of his linen pants. The sensation was so intense that he couldn't even concentrate on kissing her. He tucked her head under his chin, sank his face into her hair and prayed for a major cloud mass to pop up that would keep both pilots occupied.

"Alex," she said. She sounded breathless. She also sounded meek.

"Um?"

"May I blow my nose before we go any further with this?"

Life with Sarah, if he could manage to win her, was going to be a rocky, uncertain, twisting, uphill road. He was going to need a sturdy pair of English walking shoes.

"SOMEBODY CLEANED MY apartment." Astonished, Sarah gazed at the spotless kitchen, the tidy bed, the plumped-up sofa cushions. She'd left the kitchen counter covered with glasses and the bed in a tangle. "I know Maude didn't do it. She doesn't clean her own place until the city threatens to condemn the building. Burleigh didn't have time. Rafe?" she asked.

"I don't know his name," Alex said, "but Burleigh

said he brought reinforcements along in case you re-
sisted arrest."

"Rafe cleans?" She wished she'd gotten his phone
number. The phone number of a muscled hunk who also
cleaned house was the kind of information she ought to
pass on to Annie and Rachel.

"But can he do this?" Alex said, and did an impromptu soft-shoe routine with an imaginary top hat.

"There are lots of things you can do that Rafe can't, or
at least mayn't, not to me, anyway. Alex—" She hesitated. "Are you sure you can't stay tonight?"

He put his arms around her. "You can't imagine how
much I want to. But I really can't."

She sighed. "Just thought I'd ask."

"Next weekend?" he said.

"By next weekend," she said, looking at him thoughtfully, "I'm guessing you'll be flat on your back in bed
with my virus."

"Then it would be your turn to nurse me through it.
It's only fair."

"I suppose you're right. My place or yours?"

"If I'm well, yours. If I'm sick, mine."

"Oh, okay," she grumbled. A thought occurred to her.
"Have you heard from Libby?"

"Oh, yeah. She got a job."

"Where?" Sarah narrowed her eyes.

"Chicago."

"O'Hare," Sarah breathed.

"Excuse me?"

"Nothing," she said hastily. "Poor Macon, though. I
hope he doesn't desert me and move out there to be with
his adored one."

Alex looked uncertain. "I don't want him to get his hopes up too high. Libby spoke very highly of him, but..."

"She sees him as a makeover project."

"Something like that."

"Poor Macon," Sarah said again. "Well, would you like something to eat before you go?"

"No, I'm fine."

"A drink?"

"No, thanks."

"A back rub?" She peered up at him. He was so great to look at, absolutely irresistible in those tan slacks and cream silk shirt. He didn't need *GQ*. Or *Vogue*, either, apparently. He'd picked out the silk sundress she was wearing. She didn't want to know how much he'd paid for it. It was so hard to let him go. Too hard. Too hard for him, too, because his mouth was moving slowly down to hers.

His arms went around her. "I could stay an hour." His voice hummed in her ear, low and husky.

"Make it an hour-and-a-half?" She tugged him close and held him tight.

"You're impossible." His arms tightened, and his hands moved sensuously over her. "Give you an inch, and you'll take..."

"Eight," she said, "would be about right."

11

THE LONG, HOT SUMMER WENT by in a haze of blinding sunlight and crushing humidity, but Sarah hardly noticed. Alex was her sun, the center of her universe, gentle and life-giving.

During the week she worked hard, driving her staff to new levels of speed and perfection. The weekends were for Alex.

He didn't catch her virus, didn't end up flat on his bed feverishly coughing and snuffling in the most unattractive way. But, of course, Alex never did anything unattractive. Except bolt when you least expected it.

This summer he didn't appear to be thinking of bolting. He came to New York that next weekend and others, and all week she lived for the moment when his tall, lithe body came through her doorway and he dropped his luggage on the floor with a careless thud to free his arms so that he could throw them around her.

Some weekends she flew in the pampered luxury of his plane to San Francisco, where Alex would wait for her at his home, not wanting to share that first minute of togetherness with the pilots or Wong Li, who would pick her up at the airport. On the Fourth of July, they watched fireworks exploding over the bay from Alex's balcony, then went inside to make fireworks of their own.

Between their precious moments alone they explored the treasures of both coasts, the museums and galleries, antiques shops and wineries. They went to plays and movies, ate at interesting restaurants, met each other's friends. Alex took a day off to come to her office and get acquainted with the rest of her staff. She took a day off to visit his.

Awash with happiness and pleasure, she refused to think about the future. The *now*—that was all this was about. Alex seemed to have accepted her nonconfrontational attitude, because he hadn't mentioned love or suggested a long-term relationship in weeks.

Maybe he was no longer interested in having her back forever.

When this thought went through her head she steeled herself for a moment of utterly uncalled-for panic. She wasn't interested in forever, either, was she? Maybe everything would turn out just fine, nobody hurt, nobody the worse for a summer straight from a romance novel— without the usual ending in which the lovers rode into the sunset together. Time after time she fought down the panic, returning to the sheer delight of Alex's presence, the fun they had together, the lovemaking they shared.

Okay, so once in a while she had to take a couple of aspirin to work, to concentrate or to sleep after one of these moments of uncertainty. The day she packed for the weekend during which she would be introduced to his office staff, she observed that she was almost out of what she had supposed to be a lifetime supply of aspirin.

Even though she was still warm and fuzzy from a night of passion and fulfillment, she was nervous as all get-out when she walked into his suite of offices. After the introductions to a group of extremely pleasant, warm and interested people, a staff exactly the size of hers, she began to relax a little.

Alex ushered her into his office and glanced at his watch. "It's almost time for your appointment. I'll walk you down to the car."

On Friday, he had also made an appointment for her with his ad agency. "Russ wants to meet you," he'd told her on the phone. "He likes your work."

"You're turning out terrific stuff," said Russ Rogers, Alex's account executive. "Fresh, new, cutting-edge design."

The agency was housed in an enormous Victorian building on the edge of San Francisco's business district. Russ was easily twenty years older than she and Alex were, stout and graying, but there was a spark in his direct gaze, his alert posture, that told her he intended to be on the cutting edge for the rest of his working life. "Thank you," she said. "If we can loosen up Alex a little, I think we've got the package together."

"Alex is on the program. Don't let him con you into thinking he isn't," Russ said, surprising her. "Who are these guys who turned out the Miracle Music brochures?"

She told him about Ray and Jeremy. "If you try to hire them away from me," she said, noticing an avaricious gleam in his eye, "pay them well."

"Oh, I would never..."

"You would, too, in a New York minute."

He laughed. "Alex warned me you didn't pull any punches."

"What a thing to say," Sarah said reproachfully. "I'm

the very soul of good humor and kindness to all." She frowned. "Although I was once compared with a grass snake."

"Uh-huh." His grin widened. "Well, the bottom line is we've got more work for you if you're interested."

"I think we can fit you in, if you're not in too much of a rush," Sarah said coolly, opening the leather case that held her legal pad for making notes. She took a deep gulp of the coffee Russ had insisted on having brought to her, along with a small, rich pastry. Her heart was thudding wildly. Work! Money! Success! Raises for her staff. "What sorts of projects did you have in mind?"

Russ launched enthusiastically into a description of a promotion for a new line of bath products for children. In no time at all they were brainstorming like longtime colleagues. At last Russ ran out of steam and Sarah ran out of ideas. "Okay," Russ said. "Can you come up with a presentation by October first?"

"No problem," Sarah said confidently, and half rose to leave. She wanted to leave. She needed time to figure out how the heck her staff was going to do the work Russ had asked for in seven weeks. Was it time to hire a new person, or was that too chancy? Instinct had told her to bring along a good black pantsuit for this appointment, and now she was grateful for the way it made her feel invisible.

He leaned forward in his chair. "One more thing I want to talk to you about."

"Sure." She sat back down, perching on the very edge of her chair.

"Ever think about moving out here?"

"What?" The question shook her much more deeply

than it should have, and she was annoyed by her own reaction. "No," she said after a pause. "I'm all set up in New York. My people are New York-based. Their families are there. Why do you ask?"

"It's not Ray and Jeremy we'd like to hire. It's you."

"You have hired me."

"I mean as a member of our in-house staff—salary, benefits, perks, all that jazz."

Her reaction—surprise, suspicion, portent for the future—escalated. For some reason, she felt motivated to temper her response, to be less direct than came naturally to her. "Well, Russ, I don't know what to say. I like having my own business. My staff is loyal to me and I return that loyalty. I haven't thought about changing any of that."

"We knew you'd say that," Russ said, "and we have slots waiting for your staff. So start thinking about it." His smile was persuasive. "No need to make a decision anytime soon. We've made our offer. The details, of course, we would negotiate later, but I think you'll find them reasonable."

She edged even farther out on the chair. "And I'm so flattered by it," she assured him. "I'll...I'll..." Her rear end slipped off the chair and her body lurched a little to the left, so she stood up. "I'll give it serious thought and get back to you later. In the meantime—" she dredged up a mischievous smile "—I'll get my group onto baby soap. We'll have babies coast to coast screaming inconsolably until their mommies buy this soap."

Wong Li drove her back to Alex's office in the hub of the city. It was a beautiful city, a clean, charming and decorative city. It was a progressive city, a tolerant city.

After they'd survived the wrench of leaving New York, her staff would be happy there.

Damn it, they were happy in the dirt and the dust, the garbage and the grimy windows, the hazards of the subway, the sheer intensity of New York! *If it ain't broke, don't fix it.* But if it was broken, and she was the one to break it...

A weekend with Alex. That's what she'd come here for, and that's what she was going to focus on.

This time Wong Li had taken her bags to Alex's room, not to the guest room. Alex's household was starting to treat her like a permanent fixture. The sense of panic overcame her.

Alex was wooing her with all the components of a luxurious life, with half-spoken promises that she'd never have to lift a finger to manual labor again, never have to worry about money, never have to do anything at all if she chose not to. But if work were important to her, and she felt she'd be truly unhappy without it, Alex's ad agency would absorb everything that identified her at the moment, her and her staff.

It was, at the bottom line, something to think about. Very, very seriously.

IN EARLY AUGUST, the city had settled into a steady, complaining misery of heat and humidity. It had been a most unusual summer, without the usual breaks of cool mornings or vivid electrical storms and dark, rainy days.

ConEd, the electric company, issued grave warnings and then pious pleas to conserve power. In the suburban communities that surrounded the city, residents wa-

tered their expensive green lawns on a staggered schedule, four to six in the afternoon or eight to ten at night
like invitees to a large-scale open house.

It was Alex's turn to come to New York. Over the
phone, he worried about his social responsibility. Did he
have any right to fly in solitary luxury in his own plane,
use all that fuel for his own pleasure? Maybe he should
fly commercial. Secretly smiling, Sarah listened toler-
antly to his soul search.

In the end, several of his staff members and two California elected officials developed a sudden need to
spend the weekend in New York with their families, and
the Gotham Bar and Grill had a fresh tuna emergency
which somehow reached Alex's ears through his management analyst, Les, who was a friend of a cousin of the
wife of the chef. With the cabin packed and an extremely
large fresh fish iced down in the luggage compartment,
he was a happy man.

As always, Sarah was ready for him. Her apartment
was ready, delicious things to eat were waiting, and
above all, she was fidgety with anticipation and impatience.

He called from the plane to report his progress.
"We're making excellent time," he told her. "I should be
there by eleven your time."

She knew he was surrounded by his friends and had
to restrict himself to practical matters. But she didn't.

"I don't know how I can wait until eleven," she said,
stretching out on the sofa with a little purring noise.
"I'm so hot for you now. I'm not wearing anything but
that little black gown you like so much, remember? But I
just can't cool down."

He cleared his throat. "No break in the weather yet?" he asked rather loudly.

"Or the humidity. I'm so wet, Alex, so wet."

"We'll stay in," he said in a strangled voice. "She says the weather's awful," he reported to his audience, then returned to her. "We'll keep our cool."

"Alex, I'm telling you I don't have any cool to keep." She crossed her legs, rubbed her thighs together. Good grief. She was actually turning herself on. Lord knows what she was doing to Alex. She imagined his flushed, embarrassed face, imagined him mopping his forehead with a white linen pocket square, starched and ironed to perfection, that had his initials monogrammed in one corner. She had him right where she wanted him and he couldn't do a thing to defend himself.

"We might go up to the roof after you get here," she suggested in a throaty voice. "I'll wear what I'm wearing now, but you won't be wearing anything. You can stretch yourself out on that padded lounge chair and I'll just settle myself right on top of you, you know the way I like to wiggle myself down over you..."

"I've got Charlie the Tuna on the plane with me. Did I tell you?" He sounded desperate to change the subject.

"Is that what you're calling it now? For goodness sake, Alex, you know me too well to have to call it anything. All you have to do is use it. But I'll play your little game." She snuggled into a cushion and lapsed into baby talk. "You just tell that naughty Charlie Tuna if he'll behave himself for just a teentsy, weentsy while longer, Sarah will..."

"Make ice," he said suddenly. "Plenty of ice. I'm going to have to replace that refrigerator of yours one of these days, get you one with an icemaker. Okay, bye-bye—"

"Don't hang up! I'll stop teasing you, I promise. Alex, don't—" He disconnected the call with an abrupt snap of an end button.

She made a face at the receiver, hung up and went on waiting.

"I've said it before, I'll say it again," he began his next call. "You are a devil, a wicked tease, a—"

"Are you on the ground?"

"Yes, unfortunately. I thought about taking a helicopter, but I didn't know where to land it."

"Just hurry, okay?"

"The driver's doing his best, but he has a feeling the Yankee game has just ended. The road is packed."

The connection broke up and Sarah went back to her least favorite occupation—waiting.

And waiting, and waiting, and waiting. Eleven o'clock came, but Alex didn't.

She became aware of a commotion going on outside her windows, loud enough that she could hear it over the air conditioners. Rays of flashing light shot into the sky, slashing through her curtains. Something dramatic was happening.

This was not an unusual occurrence in New York, but it was still unnerving when whatever was happening was happening right in front of your own building.

She cracked a blind and looked out to see the street packed with police cars, fire trucks and rescue vans. Maude wouldn't be able to sleep through a racket like this. Sarah dialed her.

Maude was incoherent with excitement. In the background, Broderick barked slowly and steadily, bark, pause, bark, pause, bark. "They've treed the Village Voyeur on our block!" Maude shouted.

"At last," Sarah said. "That should restore your peace of mind."

"They've blocked off the street. Not letting anybody in or out. Gotta go. I don't want to miss anything."

Sarah segued into a serious worrying mode. How was Alex going to get here if the street was blocked? She remembered how he hated inconvenience, how frustrated he got when a schedule broke down. He was probably—

The phone rang and she snatched it up. "I'm at the bottom of your fire escape," said a deep, heavy-breathing voice.

"Who is this?" she snapped. "Get off the phone, you creep."

"Thanks a lot."

"Alex?"

"Who else would it be?"

"Why are you talking so funny?" She frowned.

"Because I don't want anybody to hear me. I really didn't call to chitchat. Please go out on your fire escape and look down."

He hung up, so she did, too. Tiptoeing barefoot out onto the fire escape, she looked down. There he was, a mere shadow at the bottom, but she had to assume it was Alex.

"Oh, poor Alex." She raced down the fire escape, got to the bottom and gazed down another twelve feet to where he stood, not as pristine as usual. His slacks were a different color halfway up his shins.

"How did you get here?" she cried down to him.

His irritation chilled the atmosphere around him. "With everything going on, I couldn't very well just show up at your front door. I went around to Thirteenth Street, slid between two buildings, climbed an eight-foot wall, landed in a child's wading pool, negotiated with a Rottweiler and then climbed another wall into the back yard of your building. Just an everyday illegal entry."

"Somebody might have killed you!" She'd been crouching on the wrought-iron landing, and now she stood up, giving him his first full view of her in her sheer black gown.

"For God's sake, Sarah, what if somebody sees you? Go back up and put on some clothes. Then we'll figure out what to do."

"Okay," she said, and raced back up the fire escape. She hopped into a pair of shorts and slid her feet into clogs. On the way back down to Alex, she pulled a tank top over her head.

"My hero," she said when she reached the bottom landing again. "You are so brave. Now all we have to do is get you up here."

He expelled an impatient sigh. "How do you undo the doodad that comes down to the ground?"

"Your weight is supposed to take the ladder down to the ground." Sarah searched the landing with her fingertips. "You have to get it started first, I guess." She pushed at the rusty ladder, pushed harder, then with an unladylike grunt, gave it all the muscle power she possessed. It didn't move.

"Then if that doesn't work," she went on, "I guess you wait for the fire department to come and rescue you.

But, of course, they're all tied up on Twelfth Street just now."

"You wouldn't be able to escape a blazing inferno until the fire department finished up on Twelfth Street?"

"Well, in the first place," she said, taking the question seriously, "I would hope the blazing inferno wouldn't coincide with a takedown on Twelfth Street. But if it did, I'd jump that far. Don't say it, I know you can't reach me by jumping." She thought for a minute. "I'll tie a sheet here at the bottom and you can climb up."

He looked at the baggage that surrounded him. "I brought flowers. Candy. Wine. Provisions."

She gazed at him. "You know what I wish you'd brought?"

He muttered, "What?"

"A fifty-four-inch television set."

"Oh, Sarah, do be serious."

"Okay, I will. Hang on a minute."

She raced up the fire escape. She hated the thought of destroying freshly, expensively laundered sheets, but in a crisis, one used what one had. She grabbed her least favorite set and went down.

"Somebody I know is certainly getting her exercise," she said cheerfully.

He glowered at her.

"Okay, okay." She tied a corner of the sheet to the railing. "See if this will hold you."

His exasperation increased. "I have to send the bags up first. You can see how important that would be. Because if I came up first, there wouldn't be anybody down here to…"

"I get it, I get it," Sarah said. "Send something up."

He tied the sheet around the cone of flowers, muttering to himself. She tugged them up. "Oh, Alex, they're gorgeous! Stargazer lilies, purple irises..."

"Send. The sheet. Back. Down."

"Oh. Sorry."

He tied the sheet to the handles of a shopping bag. This one was heavier, more awkward. She lay down flat on the landing, and after a brief struggle, managed to drag it up.

"That didn't do the wine any good," Alex said grimly from beneath her.

"I'll sing to it when I get it upstairs."

The look on his face told her he was just about fed up with her lighthearted attitude. "Now you," she told him. "Grab the sheet. Here we go. Upsy-daisy."

"You can't pull me up, Sarah. I'll have to climb."

There was no point in arguing with his logic. The shopping bag had almost done her in. She argued with him anyway. "We'll use leverage," she said. "I'll wrap the sheet around the railing. Or something. Trust me. Give it a try."

"No. You take the food upstairs and get the pâté into the fridge. I'll see you up there."

"I think I should stay. For moral support. To cheer you on." She couldn't miss the sight of Alex climbing up a sheet hand over hand.

"What you want is to see me fall flat on my ass. Now take the damned bag upstairs and let me alone."

"Oh, all right." Muttering to herself, she hoisted the bag and began the climb up the stairs. When she reached her apartment, she stuck the bag through the window and then followed it. The lights were still flashing through the slats of the blinds and making sinister patterns on the curtains as she unpacked the bag, uncovering pâté, cheese, fresh figs—somewhat squashed—more cheese, sourdough rolls...

His love in every bite. What was she going to do about Alex? What was she going to do about the feelings that swelled inside her, more powerful with each passing day?

In the near distance she heard, "Gr-oof." Pause. "Gr-oof." Pause.

For Broderick, this degree of self-expression indicated excitement that had driven him nearly out of control. A memory flashed through her mind—Burleigh bending neatly at the waist to pat Broderick on the head. They were two of a kind, Burleigh and Broderick. Still waters ran deep.

These pleasant thoughts fled when she realized that the police lights were suddenly flashing through the back windows as well as the front. A stentorian command echoed through a megaphone.

"Freeze! Hold it right there, buster."

The voice galvanized her into action. A wheel of goat cheese whirled from her grasp to the floor with an odd plopping sound as she dashed to the window, slid out onto the fire escape and looked down at the disaster below.

One of the city's finest was snapping handcuffs on Alex, and the flash of a camera added more light to the scene.

"*Village Voice,*" she heard someone say. "Chief Morrow, may we inform the public that you've finally captured the Village Voyeur?"

12

"I DON'T SEE what you're so wrought up about."

"We'll talk at home."

As soon as the police had removed his handcuffs, Alex had crossed his arms tightly across his chest, his jaw clenched, every muscle tense. At the police station he'd been standing. Now he was sitting in a taxi. Except for bending at the knees, he hadn't changed his position in the time that had elapsed.

"The taxi driver has headphones on. He won't hear a word."

"We'll talk in private."

Sarah, who sensed a fight coming on and was anxious to get it under way and finished, expelled a sigh of impatience. The sigh was merely a cover. She was holding back a serious case of the giggles. Alex and his adorable sense of dignity. He'd been sorely tested tonight. In the end, she'd had to do all the talking. He'd been, and this was a quote, "too embarrassed to call my lawyer."

She cleared her throat, the laughter so close to the surface that it sounded like a sob. He gave her a sharp glance. She looked out the window.

While she gazed at the darkened streets, it occurred to her that maybe tonight had been enough. Maybe he'd been tested enough, had sufficiently proved his love simply by wanting to be with her badly enough to try to

climb a fire escape. He hadn't blamed her when the
caper went bad, either. In fact, he hadn't introduced any
conversational topic with her at all. In hours. What she'd
always think of as his last words were, "Take the
damned bag upstairs and let me alone," unless she
counted, "We'll talk in private."

Those were not words to build dreams on. In an attempt to control herself, a snort came through her nos-
trils. The next thing she knew, a handkerchief was in her
hand. She covered her entire face with it.

"It's not funny."

Whee! Some new last words, and such appropriate
words, coming from Alex.

"Can't you see at least a little humor in the situation?"
she asked him.

"No."

It was her turn to give him a quick glance. She was
startled by the rage in his handsome face, by the glitter
in his dark eyes. No mysterious messages here. He was
furious.

He was right about one thing. This was a conversation
that had to be continued in private.

Twelfth Street was quiet at last. The Village Voyeur
had either been caught or given up on for the time being.
It was a shock to find Maude waiting for them in the
foyer. She was flanked by Broderick on her left and the
air conditioner that had been a gift from Alex on her
right. "Take it back," Maude said in a dramatic tone. "I
don't deserve it. Every day it will only remind me that
I...I..."

"That you what?" Sarah said. Alex's face was so blank

that she felt sorry for him, thought she ought to help out with the conversation.

Maude's voice sank to its lowest level, which, for Maude was very low indeed. "Betrayed you," she moaned.

"Aw, Maude, you didn't," Sarah said. "You turned Alex in as the Village Voyeur? Say it isn't so."

Maude flung out both arms in entreaty. "How was I supposed to know? I look outside and see a man climbing my fire escape, staring right through my window..."

This statement woke up the Sphinx. "I was not staring in your window."

"Looked like you were. That's all that mattered. Just think what publicity for me. 'Mystery writer Maude Coates single-handedly captured the Village Voyeur, a longtime nuisance in the downtown area of...'"

"And the publicity for me," Alex said. His tight smile was aimed at Sarah. "We'll see which one of us gets top billing in the *Voice* tomorrow."

Sarah was aware of fear beginning to grow inside her. Not fear that Alex would hit her, nothing like that. Because if he ever did, which he wouldn't, she'd just hit him back, and he knew it. This was a fear of something much deeper, that Alex was slipping away into a place where she wouldn't be able to find him. Just as he'd done twelve years ago, but this time it would be forever.

"Well, sure," Maude said, clueless. "You've got a company, right? Might give your business a boost. Name recognition, all that?" With her left hand she stroked Broderick's big, sad head, and with her right, the air conditioner. Her knees bent to reach her two most beloved possessions, she gazed up at Alex with hope in her eyes.

"I won't know until the end of the next quarter," Alex said, calm but cold. "I'll send you a report. You can see my profit/loss statement and Sarah's graphics all at the same time." He paused. "If profits are up, you keep the air conditioner. If they're down, send it back. Sarah?" He gestured her toward the elevator.

"I can't take this anymore," he said as soon as her apartment door closed behind them.

The fear grew inside her, making her want to strike back. "What exactly is it you can't take?"

"Seeing you on weekends." He began to pace the room. "Flying back and forth. Things going wrong."

Anger fixed her attention on the real truth—what Alex couldn't take was things going wrong. He was a spoiled brat who expected everything to go right for him. "I don't know what it is with you," she said. "Other people fly coast to coast all the time without getting arrested. For you, a simple plane trip is fraught with peril."

He whirled on her. "I'm trying to say something important. If you won't listen I'll stop trying."

She suddenly felt cold. She'd put on long pants to go to the precinct headquarters with Alex, but a sweater would feel good over her tank top. It was the air-conditioning. She still wasn't used to it.

"Excuse me while I get a sweater."

His eyebrows winged up and he eyed her with disbelief as she went to her bedroom and came back in a hot-pink cashmere sweater that had belonged to Aunt Becki. It had to be ten years old, and still a faint, comforting scent of Shalimar clung to it. Or did she only imagine it? "Much better now," she told him. "You were saying? Oh, would you like a glass of wine or maybe a cup of coffee while we talk? I made a yummy—"

"I'd like you to settle down and listen to me."

Feeling like a child about to be scolded, she sat on the sofa and turned her face up to him for the inevitable lecture.

From his expression, he wasn't looking forward to it. She felt a dull ache in her chest. The summer, this long, hot summer with Alex, was about to end, and not the way she'd expected.

It was startling to see Alex pull up a footstool in front of her and sit on it, to see his face soften. "I don't want to live this way anymore, Sarah. I want you with me all the time."

The ache in her heart turned into a thudding beat. No, he couldn't do this to her. He couldn't corner her, force her into a decision about him, about the two of them. She wouldn't let him.

"Come back to San Francisco with me. Come back to stay."

"Tonight?" She blinked.

"Fine with me." He actually smiled. "I was thinking Sunday. I'll arrange to have your things moved. All you'll have to do is pack a suitcase."

"All—" She was stunned. "What on earth are you talking about? What do you mean, all I have to do is pack a suitcase? I have a whole life here, not just a few clothes. I have a business, I have people who depend on me, I have clients."

Seeing her face grow pale, Alex realized he was doing

this all wrong. He'd been thinking about this conversation for a couple of weeks, feeling that she'd had time to get used to the idea of having him back in her life, and this time for keeps. He'd even had the courage to hope she was just waiting for him to say the magic words.

The magic words, of course, were *marry me*. That's how he should have started off, and would have if he hadn't been so humiliated by the experience he'd just been through. Humiliated and thoroughly ticked off at her for not recognizing his humiliation.

He was still mad about that, and mad wasn't a good way to begin a proposal. He should have said, "Marry me, and then we'll figure out how to merge our lives." Instead, he'd told her he was fed up with the status quo.

He could recoup. He had to.

"I know, I know," he said, trying to soothe her. "I didn't mean—"

"Yes, you did. That's what you said. Just pack a suitcase. Well, Alex, you're already here with a suitcase. Why don't you just stay?" She got up, futzed around straightening a flower here, a pillow there.

He'd expected her to say that. Already he felt on firmer ground, so he gave himself a moment to admire her long legs in the loose white linen pants she wore, the determined set of her narrow shoulders, the cloud of blond hair that felt like satin between his fingers. "That's always an option," he said.

"An option? Another option is for you to get over this little *thing* that happened tonight so we can have a nice weekend and go on to have more nice weekends together."

"*Little thing?* You mean you saw that article in the paper about my mother and still can't understand that to me this wasn't a *little thing?* Me, in police custody, with reporters taking pictures? No better than my mother! It wasn't a little thing, Sarah, it was my nightmare coming true."

He felt that his anger was justified, and still he knew he should have given himself a minute to calm down, then apologized for taking out his frustration on her. But hell, wouldn't anybody be upset about being taken for the guy who'd been peeking at women through windows? Wouldn't anybody be upset about being hauled off to jail? About the possibility of having his picture plastered across the pages of a scandal sheet? Well, okay, it didn't seem to bother his mother, but any normal person?

Damn straight they would! What right did Sarah have to make him feel like a stuffy prig when his reaction was the normal one?

"Your nightmare? Well, let me tell you about my nightmare."

Too late, he realized he'd made her madder than he was emotionally capable of getting. Her passion, which stirred his emotions to life, was as intense in anger as it was in joy.

"My nightmare," she said, her voice thin with barely controlled fury, "is that I would believe all your pretty words and declarations of devotion, put myself in your hands and then watch you drop me. Again. Don't you think I'd be stupid to do that, Alex? Don't you think it would be pretty nearsighted of me to give up a life I've built here and go out to California with you, when I might find myself stranded there at any minute?"

"I would never do that."

"Your mother has done it over and over and over!"

"I'm not my mother."

"How can I be sure of that?"

"Nobody can ever be sure of anything. All I know is that I love you. I want you in my life. I'll help you reestablish your own company, or you can work for Russ—"

"You've already set it up, haven't you?" Her eyes were even wilder than before. "You've taken it upon yourself to find jobs for my whole crew if they want them. You've probably even found office space for me if I insist on running my own business. You've built a trap, and all I have to do is fall into it."

A trap! "It wouldn't have been responsible of me to ask you to move if I didn't have a clear picture of—"

"Well, listen to this, Alex. I've been in control of my own life for a long time now. I don't need anybody to set me up in a pretty little house or a pretty little office. I saw how Aunt Becki lived, and I swore I'd never put my whole existence under some man's control, certainly not yours. I won't be told where to live or how to live. I'm happy just the way I am. With you or without you!"

He was more capable of anger, more able to be hurt than he'd realized. "Fine," he said, too upset to care about the finality of it all. "Try it without me for a while."

She could have stopped him with one word, could have pulled him back into her life the way she did that night in early June, but she didn't.

A MAJOR POLICE EFFORT to apprehend the so-called Village Voyeur, a Peeping Tom who has been a Greenwich Village an-

noyance for several years, was aborted tonight when police
mistook a visitor from San Francisco for the Voyeur. The vis-
itor was attempting to reach a friend who was expecting him.
Unable to enter on Twelfth Street due to the police block, he
was climbing the fire escape when a neighbor reported him. Af-
ter a brief questioning, he was released....

Several blocks west, Macon, Annie and Rachel stared
at the television set in the not-at-all-trendy bar where
they'd stopped for a nightcap after seeing a movie together. "That's Alex," Rachel exclaimed.

"Golly," Annie said. "Poor Alex. Sarah says he's so
proper about everything."

Macon swore under his breath. "I have a feeling about
this."

"What sort of feeling?" Rachel said. "Be specific."

"This incident will bring matters to a head," Macon
said.

"Between Sarah and Alex."

"Yes."

"They're going to break up?" Rachel seemed to see
the future of the office and clearly found it depressing.

"No," Annie said, and sighed. "They'll get married
and live happily ever after."

"The question, Annie, is where?"

"Oh, in a church, or maybe they'd rather—"

"Macon meant where are they going to live happily
ever after," Rachel said, her edgy voice contrasting with
Annie's dreamy one. "Here or in San Francisco."

Annie frowned. "I hadn't thought about that."

"You'd better start thinking about it." Rachel gave
Macon a grim glance. "I don't know how I could move.
The expense, for one thing, but that's nothing compared

to my family. They'd go ballistic. A Sokolov doesn't leave Brooklyn on a whim. Heck, a Sokolov doesn't move off Twenty-First Street in Midwood without a going-away party."

"You wouldn't get a kick out of being the first Sokolov nomad?" Macon asked her. "The leader of the Sokolov diaspora?"

"The what?" Annie said.

"Fuhgeddaboudit," Rachel muttered.

"I spent my last penny moving here," Annie said.

"Don't take out a loan until we see what happens," Macon said.

"You offering low interest rates?" Rachel wanted to know.

"The lowest," Macon assured her. "Another drink, ladies? My treat."

SARAH NOTICED the odd looks she got from her staff when she came in on Monday morning. She thought she'd pulled herself together pretty well for a person who'd been crying all weekend, but something was tipping them off. Maybe it was the way she'd crawled in rather than pranced.

She endured the solicitous way they stepped around her, didn't ask her any questions, didn't stop in to chat and, when talking among themselves, they spoke in low voices, until four o'clock that afternoon. Then she called them all in.

"It's over," she said. "I know it's a personal matter and no one's business but mine, but we've become such good friends that I—"

"Oh, no," Annie said, looking stricken.

"Oh, yes. Alex had a little problem getting to my apartment Friday night, so he did this whole 'I can't take it anymore' thing. Said I had to move to San Francisco."

They were scarily silent.

"He assured me I could bring all of you with me. We have jobs assured at Sweeney and Swain if we want them."

The only response she got from them was a set of blank stares.

"I told him in no uncertain terms how I felt about *that*," she said next.

"About what?" Annie said.

"About him taking control of my life. About him calling all the shots. I mean, how do I know how he'll feel about me a year from now? One of his mother's marriages lasted four days."

"What did he say?" Annie seemed to be the only member of her staff who hadn't been struck dumb.

"He left."

"Oh."

"I just wanted you to know." She made an effort to sound chipper. "We still have the Emerson Associates projects to finish. Let's be sure to do our best work for them. That is all." She stood up.

As they filed out, still giving her those *looks*, she called Macon back. "Is that shirt silk?" she asked him.

He blushed. "The tag said it was."

"Was this silk shirt an independent decision?"

"No," he admitted.

"Libby picked it out?"

"She offered to help me. We went shopping a few

times. But take off that Valentine face," he said. "We decided just to be friends."

"Oh," Sarah said sorrowfully. "Was it painful?"

"I hope not," Macon said. "I tried to break it to her as gently as possible."

Sarah couldn't help gasping at the thought that Macon had ditched Libby and not the other way around.

"We didn't have much in common," Macon explained. "She doesn't know a docking station from a surge protector. Besides, she's moving to Chicago."

Sarah narrowed her eyes. "You didn't care enough about her to commute?"

"Not all the airlines have plugs under the seats for laptops," Macon said. "Sarah, what are you—" He got out the door before Sarah's tissue box could connect with his head.

ALEX SLUMPED over his keyboard, staring at the spread in the New York *Daily News.* He hadn't even known a *News* reporter was in the melee at the foot of Sarah's fire escape, but one must have been, because there he was, Alex Emerson, in full color, wearing handcuffs.

He'd done the right thing by walking out. No woman was worth that kind of embarrassment, even Sarah.

She was too demanding.

She was still angry after all these years. He'd never be able to change her mind about him. He'd only be dealing himself sorrow to try. How could he have made it any clearer that he didn't want her to control her, he just loved her?

At once he thought of a couple of dozen ways, but he

shut his mind off to the possibilities. It was over. He'd given it a try, and he'd failed.

He'd had no idea she identified so closely with her aunt, had such a fear of finding herself in the same help-less situation. That could never happen to Sarah. She was too strong. Too strong even for him.

That was Monday. The closer he came to the time he would have been getting on the plane and jetting off to the delights of Sarah, the more he wondered if he hadn't overreacted. If he'd said, "I'm sorry. I was wrong to try to reorganize your life. I'll reorganize mine," they might have—

They might have gone on exactly as they were un-til...until when? Until she finished his projects? Until she could separate business from pleasure?

He couldn't have stood the uncertainty much longer anyway. Walking out when she said she was happy with him or without him had been for the best. In the long run, anyway.

That was Thursday. By the following Monday, he was a madman. He could only think of one thing to do to make himself feel closer to her. It was pathetic, really, but he did it anyway. He picked up the phone.

"Russ," he said, "I've got a couple of new companies I need to pitch to investors."

"WHO?" SARAH SAID, trying to rouse herself from the lethargy she'd fallen into.

"El-ea-nor As-quith." When Rachel whispered, her voice was hardly recognizable.

Sarah froze to her chair. "Are we on the speaker-phone?"

"No." Rachel raised her voice to normal range.

"Is she armed?"

"Just a few minutes of your time, she says."

Rachel hadn't answered her question about weapons, and a few minutes were plenty of time to fire and run. Sarah heard the hum of other voices behind Rachel's. "Is she flanked by troops?"

"Ray and Jeremy are with her now. If you're pushed for time, they could continue to entertain her until you're available." The words were loaded with meaning. Ray and Jeremy were fawning over the famous film star. Jeremy was probably quoting lines from her last movie while doing a passable impression of her elegant voice, or even, horror of horrors, flouncing around the room doing an impression of her entire screen persona.

"Dear God." Sarah bit her lip. "Send her in. No!" she said swiftly. "Show her in. Offer her tea. Break open the cookies we save for the high-end clients. Rachel—"

"What?"

"Be excessively formal. Do you understand the concept?"

After a brief pause, Rachel said, "Yes, ma'am."

Eleanor Asquith showing up now was the last straw. Why was she here? To gloat? To pretend to console Sarah for losing her son a second time? Rage made Sarah's scalp prickle. She wondered where Rachel kept the drain cleaner and how she could slip a little—no, a lot, best not to take any chances, the woman was made of steel—into her tea.

All summer, she'd had the loose, languid, floaty feeling of ice cream melting in the heat. It was almost a relief to be suddenly transformed into a Popsicle, a crisp, crunchy stick of—lemon would do it—lemon ice. Sugar-free.

The door wafted open as if moved by spirits, and the great lady—or the naughty lady, depending on your point of view—stepped regally in.

"Sarah." Eleanor Asquith came to a dead halt, opened her beautiful aquamarine eyes wide, then held out a long, graceful hand. "My dear," she said in that memorable voice, "you were an exquisite teenager. You are even more beautiful now. What a pleasure to see you after all these years."

Sarah sneaked a glance behind her to see if someone else might be in the room, someone Eleanor might consider it a pleasure to see again after all these years. Of course, there wouldn't be. "Good afternoon, Lady Forsythe," she said politely.

"Not anymore," Eleanor said.

"Miss Asquith, then. How kind of you to call."

Where did that come from? Fending off a curtsy her knees threatened to perform all by themselves, she added, "Please have a seat. May my assistant bring you a cup of tea? Coffee?"

"We're adults now. Surely you can call me Eleanor." Looking perfectly cool and poised in a mint-green, identifiably Chanel suit on this ninety-seven-degree day, the woman slid lightly onto a guest chair, crossed slim, elegant knees and ran a hand over her perfectly smooth blond chignon. "I've grown quite fond of that drink you Americans have taken to, the iced tea in a bottle that's so sweet and lemony. The diet version. Would you have that available?"

No, but the deli downstairs and next door would. "Of

course," she murmured, and picked up the phone. "Rachel, Miss Asquith would like a diet iced tea. I'll have—" she thought about it for a second "—I'll have a Raspberry-Peach Mountain Dream," hoping Rachel would interpret the request as a cry for help.

"You've gone over the edge," Rachel muttered.

"Yes," Sarah said sweetly. "And can we lower the AC just a notch?"

"Lower the AC? You know it won't go any lower. Do you need to see a doctor now or can you hold on a while?"

"As quickly as possible, please.

"So, Eleanor," she said, hoping she sounded smooth and, if possible, patronizing, "what brings you to New York in this dreadful weather?"

"My son's well-being."

This abrupt statement ended all hope Sarah had for finessing her way through an awkward situation. "Has something happened to Alex?"

"He's lost you. Again. I understand he's inconsolable."

Alex. Inconsolable. "Surely that's overstating it a bit."

"He applied to the Foreign Legion."

Sarah gazed at the woman opposite her, a woman of enormous power and self-assurance, a consummately selfish woman, who, Sarah now distinctly recalled, had had hazel eyes, not vivid blue-green, twelve years ago. "You made up that part," she said.

"Yes. If Alex had chosen to go into military service, he surely would have chosen the Navy. Such elegant uniforms. But my point is the same. I understand he's unhappy and since I feel somewhat responsible for it—"

she paused for a deep and dramatic sigh "—I decided to talk with you."

"You keep saying 'I understand he' instead of 'he is.' How do you know he's unhappy?"

Eleanor's eyes shifted briefly away. "I have my sources."

Sarah leaned across her desk, as much for support as anything else. The idea that had just crossed her mind made her feel shaky with anger. "Does Burleigh report to you?"

"Burleigh!" The smooth, lovely face contorted, to the extent it could after, apparently, its history of face-lifts. "That traitorous toad." Her voice actually trembled. "I don't speak to Burleigh and never will again!"

"Libby?" What she felt now was very different from anger. "Is Alex seeing Libby?"

"Oh, for heaven's sake, no. I gave it a try, as you know, but it didn't work."

It seemed Eleanor had spent all the emotion of which she was capable.

"Then who's telling you these things about Alex?" Sarah, who hadn't even tapped her wellspring of emotion, spat out the words.

"Um," Eleanor hummed. "Well, I suppose I did assist the Wongs just a trifle in getting their family to the States."

"Get out of my office!" Wow, that had felt wonderful. "How dare you invade Alex's privacy like that! You've never been close to him, never been a real mother to him. He's old enough to take care of himself now, so why can't you stay the hell out of his life!"

"Because I care about him."

"Care about him!"

"Tea, anyone?"

"No," Sarah yelled at Rachel. "What do you mean, care about him. You never—"

"Yes, please," Eleanor said. "Thank you, Rachel. So kind of you."

"—cared about him before!"

"I brought you some plain iced tea," Rachel said. "I knew you didn't want that swill you ordered. May I offer you a cookie, Miss Asquith?"

"Burleigh brought him up! And did a damned fine job of it! A better job than any of those boy toys you kept bringing home could have done."

"These look lovely," Eleanor said, lifting a cookie in her perfect fingertips. "Umm, so buttery and delicious."

Sarah lowered her voice to a growl. "You don't deserve to care about the man Alex grew up to be. You had nothing to do with it."

"If there's nothing more you need," Rachel said.

"No, dear, that will be all," Eleanor said.

"No, dear, that will not be all! Take this woman away. Get her out of my sight! At once!" But her words echoed off the closed door. Vibrating with fury, she stared at Eleanor Asquith and suddenly realized who she was, what she was, and the awful, angry words she had just uttered.

She slumped against her desk, her rage abated, reality returning in a painful rush. "Oh, Eleanor, what are we doing here? What am I saying? How can I have behaved so badly? It *would* be best if you left. I seem to have lost—"

"You have done two things, Sarah," Eleanor said,

feathering her fingers over a cocktail napkin. "You have paid me the compliment of not treating me with the deference one should show to an *older* woman, and you've convinced me you really do love my son."

"What?" A really bad headache was throbbing at the back of her skull. She sank back into her chair and closed her eyes, hoping the whole scene would vanish when she opened them.

"I assumed it was puppy love when you were teenagers. I saw my son's life heading for ruin, a marriage too early, babies, regrets, heartbreak, divorce..."

"Like you."

"Well, yes. I saw no need for Alex to make the same mistakes I did."

"We wouldn't have made that mistake." Now tears were throbbing back there with the headache. She would not cry in front of this woman. She absolutely would not.

"You thought you wouldn't, but things happen. My son deserved an education, a chance to make more mature choices. I was determined he would have that."

"He deserved a mother, too, and the kind of stepfather who could make up for the loss of his own father."

"Sarah. It's not possible to change history." For a moment Eleanor's mouth formed a pout. "He could have had a marvelous time with me and the stepfather-of-the-moment if he hadn't been such a stuffy little boy."

"Stuffy! Alex isn't stuffy. He's reserved. He—"

"Doesn't know how to laugh. Especially at himself."

"He laughs with me." Too late, Sarah realized she'd used the present tense.

"He's in love with you."

"Not anymore. It's over. Finished. Which is why I find it so peculiar that you're here. Now. After it's over. I'm not making myself very clear, am I? What I'm trying to say is that I didn't want to have this little talk with you when Alex and I were together. Why should I want to have one now that it's over?"

"It doesn't matter whether you wanted to," Eleanor said with a show of great patience. "I wanted to, so we are."

"And why, Eleanor, why did you want to?" She was getting mad again and couldn't help herself. "I wasn't good enough for the Asquith-Emerson line twelve years ago, so why am I suddenly a prospect now?"

"Oh, Sarah, it was never that you weren't good enough for my son." Eleanor's eyes widened. "If anything, I felt my son wasn't old enough to behave responsibly toward you."

Sarah's mouth dropped open. "What?"

"That's right. I found Todd Haynes's behavior toward your aunt appalling. He worshipped her, adored her, but couldn't handle a little upheaval in his life in order to make his love for her public. I was afraid my son might grow up to be just such a person, and you deserved better. A woman wants love, but she also needs to feel in control of her own decisions."

Sarah knew how stupid she must look, simply staring at the woman, but she was too startled to say a word. What Eleanor had just said was too much like her own angry speech to Alex.

"He's grown into a fine man, and I'm here to ask you to give him a second chance."

"Third." She wasn't too stupefied to keep the record straight.

"All right, third." Eleanor stood, giving every indication she was ready to leave.

A few minutes ago Sarah would have welcomed the signs. Now she felt unwilling to let Eleanor go with so much left unsaid. Nor was Eleanor quite through.

"Neither of you is complete without the other," she told Sarah almost gently. "I waited, I admit, until I was sure, and now I am. It's an enviable position, Sarah. Few people are lucky enough to find the person who is truly his other half. God knows I never did." She smiled. "I wanted a better life for you than your aunt's. I also wanted a more fulfilling personal life for my son than I have had." With a wave of her hand, she made a perfectly timed exit.

Sarah felt dizzy, frustrated—Eleanor had gotten the last word, for one thing—but wondered if Eleanor might be right. Was Alex her other half?

She was the chimera, he was the reality. She was the adventurer, Alex was...home.

It felt terrible being homeless.

13

"WE CAN DO IT if we have to."

"She says it's all over with Alex. Why should I even be worrying myself about it?"

"She doesn't mean it. It's not over. You'll see."

"I still can't go."

"You can so, Rachel. If Ray and I can part from our gorgeous houseplants and our friends, who are already making sob sounds about no more of our fabulous Halloween parties, you can separate from your tiresome family. What are you, thirty? Way past textbook separation time. In fact..."

"Your frigging houseplants don't equal my family." Rachel drew her verbal sword.

"Rachel. Jeremy." Macon took back the chairpersonship of this impromptu meeting. They were meeting in his apartment. It was his right. "No fighting, please. We have big decisions to make here."

"I just kissed my boyfriend for the first time," Annie said, looking woeful.

They all turned to stare at her. "After how many dates?" Ray said.

Annie pursed her lips. "So I'm a little old-fashioned. Well, so is he."

"So is Alex," Rachel said.

"Which suggests that when they work through this little tiff they're having, Sarah might decide to join him in San Francisco and we need to be ready for it. But personality traits aside," Macon said with all the force he could muster, "if we did it, how would we do it?"

"I haven't a nickel," Annie said.

"What you would have is an assured job," Macon said. "Russ Rogers wants to hire all of us unless Sarah is determined to set up her own shop. One way or the other, our futures look good. All we have to think about is now."

"We could rent a van and all of us could drive together to San Francisco," Annie ventured, although she still looked sad. "That would take care of plane fares."

"I could store my stuff with Mama and Papa," Rachel said. Grudgingly, but she said it.

"We can ship and fly, Jer, but it would be more fun to drive with the group," Ray said, looking at Jeremy's horrified expression.

"Oh, I guess," Jeremy grumbled. His eyes brightened. "We could make space for a couple of my cacti in the van, couldn't we?"

"I'm sure we could," Macon said. "Okay, Rachel, you check out the van. I'll get on the computer tonight and look for rentals. We could start by renting a big house for all of us. I'll shoulder the initial costs." He thought about it, because of course he could easily afford to do whatever he wanted, if he could only figure out what he wanted. "I might even buy one of those big white-elephant Victorians. As your salaries started coming in, you could make a choice to stay or find your own places."

"We really could do this," Annie said, breathless.

"If we had to. And you, Annie, would have the awesome responsibility of moving the company. Ray and Jeremy—"

"We have to fulfill our current contracts."

"Right," Macon said. "Including the flood of work that has just come in from Russ Rogers."

"IS HE GONE?" Mike said.

"Yes," Carol said, collapsing gracelessly into a chair at the conference table. "I thought I'd never get rid of him."

"Is it just a cleaning?"

"Yes." Carol gave him a shifty look. "But the dental technician is my cousin Shelley. She's going to find *things*, things that require the dentist to take a look. She's engaged to the dentist, and if all goes well, he'll hum and haw and suggest X rays. I'd say we have a couple of hours."

"That's plenty of time," Mike said. "This should be easy enough. Okay, Suzi, this is your day in the sun. How do we run the firm out of San Francisco if Alex moves to New York?"

Suzi was ready with the technological information and the cost figures. As Mike had said, it would be easy enough. All it took was money to buy the technology. The firm had plenty of that. What it didn't have at the moment was a leader running at full steam. Each person at the conference table knew he wouldn't run at full steam until he was reunited with Sarah.

Sarah had their united stamp of approval. She was just what Alex needed, what Alex had apparently needed all the time they'd been in his employ. She was beautiful, genuine, sensitive, and had always been as much in love with Alex as he'd been with her.

They liked their jobs. They loved Alex, their friend, their surrogate son, their boy genius. He'd figure out himself sooner or later that Sarah was the only thing missing in his life, and when he did, they'd be behind his decision to join her in New York one-hundred percent.

What would the office be like without Alex? Each of them, thinking about Alex's current mood, thought it would be...wonderful.

A crashing sound alerted them that the meeting had come to an end. It was only Alex opening and closing the tall outer door of the office suite, but these days he gave this simple act his own signature twist. Before they could melt quietly into their separate offices, he loomed up behind them in the doorway.

"Muu-ut-ny?" he said indistinctly.

"Oh, Alex," Carol said. "What happened to you?"

"'Ad to 'ave a fii-ing," Alex muttered.

"A filling!"

The five members of Alex's team exchanged glances, each wondering the same thing. Would a dentist's love for his fiancée drive him to fill a tooth that didn't need filling, just to extend his patient's appointment time?

It was unlikely, but then, love was a pretty powerful thing.

Their glances sent another message, as well. "Sit down, Alex," Mike said. "We have something to talk to you about."

"How can we get all this work done on time?" One glance at Annie's timetable was enough to drive Sarah to despair.

"I can't work any harder." Jeremy was near tears.

"When did you get here this morning?"

"We didn't leave last night."

Sarah looked at Ray's haggard face. She'd taken a project home with her and had awakened this morning with her laptop askew in the bed beside her and a truly unique brochure layout on the monitor.

Her shop was falling apart. Russ Rogers from Alex's ad agency called almost every day to offer Great Graphics! more work. This was clearly her path to success and she couldn't bring herself to tell him they didn't have the manpower for more projects. Ray and Jeremy were teaching Annie and Rachel to do things that went well beyond their job descriptions and skill levels. They'd even made a stab at letting Macon write some copy. It was surprisingly good.

They were pulling together, and still they were falling apart. They were getting rich, but at this rate, wouldn't live to spend it.

"Give everybody bonuses," Sarah told Annie sometime later. "I don't have time to work out new salary contracts."

"You need to hire another artist and another gofer," Annie said.

"I know that's what I need to do, but what if the boom doesn't last?" Sarah said. "Apparently Alex doesn't know Russ is giving us all this work or he'd put a stop to it."

"I don't think he'd do something that low," Annie said, jutting her chin out stubbornly.

Sarah sighed. "Maybe not."

"Maybe Russ is trying to convince us to go to work for the agency. You and Ray and Jeremy would have the support of a large company instead of trying to do it on your own."

"I like having my own company." Sarah tightened up her chin, too, and tried to stare Annie down.

"Then you need to hire more people."

"I don't have time to interview applicants."

"Rachel has an unemployed cousin."

"Bring her on," Sarah said, not even bothering to inquire about the field in which the cousin was unemployed.

"Him," Annie said.

"Whatever." Sarah no longer had the energy to stare down even the gentle, romantic Annie. She was tired of worrying, tired of squelching thoughts of Alex, tired of wondering what he was up to. His mother said he was inconsolable, but she didn't believe it for a minute.

"MAKE SOMETHING UP," Alex told Russ Rogers. "I want her so loaded down with work she won't have time to get into any mischief." Like running away. Like relocating her shop, changing her name, vanishing again before he had a chance to make up for his stupidity.

"I've already given her more than she can handle."

"That's the beauty of the situation. Doesn't matter if she gets it finished or not, since I don't need it anyway."

"Alex, you're blowing money right and left!"

"And I'm just getting started," Alex said. He felt better every minute now that he was moving forward. Not merely forward but east, east to New York to be with Sarah. He'd been a fool to try to take charge of her life, a life she'd been in charge of since Becki died. She loved him. He'd never been surer of anything in his life. All he had to do was think of a way to prove to her that he loved her even more.

It would come to him eventually, the way to do that. Moving east was only the first step.

"Will I see you at the opera Saturday night?" Russ

said, apparently giving up on talking sense to a madman.

"No. I'm going to New York tomorrow. House-
hunting."

RACHEL'S COUSIN Bart was an MBA who'd been down-
sized. He was interviewing and would undoubtedly
land a job soon, but in the meantime, he was bored. He
seemed to be enjoying the bustle of Sarah's beleaguered
office and cheerfully made coffee, answered the phone,
lifted things, cleaned and made deliveries. When he
couldn't find anything else to do, he quietly surfed the
Internet on his own computer, which he'd set up in a
corner of the central workroom.

"This is weird," he said one day.

Six pairs of eyes turned on him. The new rule during
their work crisis was no chitchat, and until this moment,
he'd followed it to the letter. It was Jeremy who finally
spoke. "What's weird?"

"I was revising Annie's timetable," Bart said, "and I
got curious about our new clients."

The room hummed with noises. Sarah wasn't paying
Bart to get curious. Getting coffee—that was his real job.

"So I looked up the first couple of companies," Bart
went on, oblivious to the general discontent with his ac-
tivities, "and this Emerson guy Rachel told me about
owned an interest in both of them, which made me even
more curious."

"What?" Sarah said. She'd been working hard, too.
With no need to go out and make sales, she was spending all her time on the work she really loved, actually designing. But Bart had gotten her full attention.

"I thought it was too much of a coincidence, so I kept
going. He owns the controlling interest in all of these
companies we're doing the promotional materials for."

She stood up, shaky and faint. "Alex generated all this new business?"

"See," Annie said, "I told you he had our best interests at heart."

"Or not," Sarah yelled. They all jumped. "What if he's—what if he's conning me into believing we're an overnight success, into hiring more people, and then, *boom*."

"Boom?" Macon frowned.

"Boom he takes the business away, leaving me with a payroll I can't meet, no new contacts because I've been too tied up with his stuff to sell our services. I'm ruined. He, on the other hand, has had his revenge."

"Oh, my," Ray said. "Never thought of that."

"Well, he would." Sarah gritted her teeth. "And I'm going to track him down and ask him just what he's up to. Rachel?"

"I'm dialing," Rachel said. "Take the call in your office."

"Hi, Sarah," Carol said.

"Where is he?"

"Alex?"

"Of course Alex." She was fuming with anger.

"I'm sorry, he's out of town until Tuesday."

"Where out of town? Or are you sworn to silence?"

"He's in New York, actually. Let's see... Right about now he'd be at Eleven Seventy-Second Street. You might try to reach him on his cell—"

Sarah was already out the door. She wouldn't call him. She'd go to Eleven Seventy-Second Street and beard him in whatever den he'd crept into.

Her devoted team watched her leave. "This is all my fault," Bart said.

"Don't worry about it," Jeremy said. "It was bound to come to a head sooner or later."

"What did you find out about the van, Rachel?" Macon asked.

"You think we're moving?"

"I think we ought to be ready."

"Where are we moving?" Bart said.

"San Francisco."

"May I come, too?"

"We'd love to have you," Annie said generously.

"It would take the heat off me with the family," Rachel said. "Okay, here's what I found out. If we reserve the van with a deposit now, we'll get a big discount."

"Let's do it," Ray said.

"Wait until Sarah gets back," Macon suggested. "I have a feeling we'll know for sure then."

"THIS IS THE MOST gracious home on the current market," said the real-estate agent. "Just steps off Fifth Avenue and park views from the fourth and fifth floors. One of our recent buyers turned the fifth-floor ballroom into a solarium, all glass on the Central Park side. It's quite—"

"It's available immediately?"

"Yes. The price—"

"May the interior design firm come in on Monday?"

"We can arrange that, yes. We'd require a—"

"How fast can you draw up the papers?"

"Could I answer the door first?"

It seeped into Alex's focused brain that the doorbell was, in fact, ringing and had been ringing incessantly for the last minute or so. "If it's an interested buyer, tell him the house is sold."

"That's wonderful, Mr. Emerson. You won't be sorry.

The house has such lovely proportions, and such a beautiful little backyard. It's a very special—"

"Will you answer the damned door? It's driving me crazy."

The agent scurried away and Alex contemplated the house he'd just committed to buy. The first floor held a kitchen, a formal dining room and a sizeable bedroom and bath that could be made into a pleasant home for Burleigh.

Burleigh claimed to be looking forward to the move. The Wongs—Alex's jaw tightened—would be staying in San Francisco with their family, whom, he'd just learned, his mother had had a hand in moving to the States.

His mother had just shocked the hell out of him by announcing that she'd had a woman-to-woman chat with Sarah and could assure him Sarah could easily be won if only Alex would stop being so stuffy. Not only was Alex furious with her for choosing this odd moment to interfere in his life, he also didn't believe her.

To calm down, he returned his attention to his surroundings. On the second floor, a living room stretched the full length and narrow width of the town house. When he owned the house, he'd turn one end into a library with big French doors opening out onto the small, perfect garden that lay between the main house and the garage and quarters for domestic staff. The third floor and the fourth, where he was now, were bedroom floors large enough to house a family, with wrought-iron balconies at the back. Last there was the fifth-floor ballroom, a practical addition when the house was built in 1890, but now, the idea of a solarium appealed to—

Shouting voices two floors below him woke him up from a dream of having coffee and reading the paper with Sarah in his new solarium. Some nut must have been at the door and was now attacking the real-estate agent. He supposed it was his job to save her.

Dashing from the room, he ran smack-dab into Sarah.

The impact knocked the breath out of him. Behind Sarah, the agent babbled. "I'm so sorry, Mr. Emerson, I couldn't stop her."

"Just what do you think you're doing?" Sarah's big blue eyes were wild, her hair was wild, her slim black dress needed to be tugged down and twisted around so that the front was actually in the front. She was the most beautiful sight he'd ever seen, and the maddest.

"Buying a house," he said when he got his breath back. "Like it? It needs a lot of work, of course, but—"

"I'll tell you what you can do with your damned house," she yelled at him, not even slightly winded from climbing three sweeping flights of stairs and running into a wall of flesh. "I mean what are you doing to my business!"

"Growing it. That's what I do. I make businesses grow."

She flung her handbag to the other side of the room. "Just listen to you! I'm having a nervous breakdown and you stand there all calm and contained telling me about growing businesses! Why did you give me all this work, that's what I came here to find out."

"Maybe I should go back to my office and draw up those papers, Mr. Emerson," the agent said.

"I don't give a damn what you do at your office," Sarah informed her at the top of her voice. "Just leave. This is private."

"Lock up when you leave," the agent threw over one shoulder as she scurried away. "I'll expect to see you at—"

"You'll see him when I get through with him, if he's still alive when I get through with him!"

Dear God, how he loved her. She was so cute right now he wanted to smile at her, but an inner voice told him it was not the time to smile. Or to tell her how cute she was.

It was time to show her how he felt about her. And he still didn't know how he was going to do that. Upending his own life, doing business at long distance, setting up housekeeping in her town, none of these things would be enough, not for Sarah.

Because Sarah, with all her bluster, was the sweetest, softest, kindest and most loving person on earth, and all it had netted her so far was pain. The pain of her parents' untimely death. The pain not only of Becki's death, but of observing her life, the compromises she'd made, and Sarah's fear of being too much like her aunt. The pain of his betrayal. Pain had made her strong. It had also made her needy. It was up to him to convince her he could meet that need, all her needs, forever and ever.

"Well?" Sarah said. Her face was red with heat and anger.

Something she'd said to him on their last, disastrous night together crossed his mind. *Can't you find anything at all funny about this situation?*

Ah, Sarah, how the worm has turned.

That, of course, made him the worm.

Good Lord, he did have a sense of humor, and no sooner did he locate it than he was being forced to control it. Life wasn't fair.

"I'm moving to New York."

"Why?"

"To be closer to you."

"Ha!" Sarah said. "To be in a better position to control my life. Look what you've already done. You've tied us up so completely with your work that I don't have time to work on new prospects or make sales! And don't think I don't know why." She shook a threatening fist at him.

"Why?" he said.

"So you can suddenly take it away and ruin me!"

"No, that's not why at all." It was time now, it really was time, to take charge of something, like this conversation. "I wanted you to be·too committed to run away from me again."

"You expect me to believe that?"

"Yes." The scene no longer struck him as funny. "Sarah—"

"Well, I don't. You've even got your mother trying to change my mind."

"I had nothing to do with my mother's visit, but I apologize for it anyway. Sarah—"

"And look what you're doing here." Whirling, she moved out onto the fourth-floor balcony. He followed, ready to grab her if she tried to jump. Looking down, his eyes followed the curve of a huge old wisteria vine that climbed all the way to the roof. Its blooms were spent now, but next spring...

"Buying the biggest house in New York," she ranted, "and pretending you're doing it to be closer to me. What you're doing is making it impossible for me to go on with my life. Why couldn't you just stay where you belong?"

In the yard next door, an elegant lunch party was taking place. Alex wished she'd lower her voice.

So he lowered his. "Because we belong together, and if you'll give me a chance to prove it, we can—"

"What's the matter, Alex? Are you afraid the neighbors will hear us fighting? Well, let them. Let them hear me tell you that we belonged together years ago, but not anymore." Her eyes filled with tears he hadn't expected. "I admit I was having second thoughts, wondering if I'd overreacted, but this threat to my business confirmed it for me."

"Threat to your business? There was no threat to your business! Damn it, Sarah, I can't even have a conversation with you. I don't know how."

He couldn't handle another minute of this. He was so frustrated, felt so impotent, that if he stayed around, he'd say something he'd regret forever. Without a backward glance, he strode off the balcony, down the stairs and out the front door.

Two steps down the sidewalk, he halted. Damn it, he was not going to give up. He was not going to lose Sarah. She didn't even want to be lost! Filled with new vigor for the fight, he spun on one heel, went up the stoop and applied a heavy hand to the big brass doorknob.

The door had locked behind him.

For a moment he stared at it. He could ring the bell. She wouldn't answer. He could pound the huge brass knocker straight through the wood. She'd pay no attention. He drew back his fist and slammed it into the door.

He knew at once he'd broken at least one knuckle. The pain cleared his mind. The solution came to him in a powerful rush—how he could prove to Sarah that he loved her, that he was capable of change and she was the only woman in the world who could give him the incentive to change.

Protecting his wounded hand as best he could, he scaled the locked wrought-iron gate that led to the backyard.

THERE WAS NO FURNITURE in the house, so Sarah was sobbing against a soiled wall. All she'd had to do was keep her temper under control and let go of her stupid pride. She could have gotten Alex back with one word, one smile, one hug.

All she had to do was forgive.

Her cell phone rang, and she made a dash for the handbag she'd thrown on the floor. It would be Alex and this was her chance, maybe her last chance, to make up her mind. Love him or leave him, just the way he'd left her all those years ago.

"They caught the Village Voyeur!"

Maude's voice, not Alex's, came on the phone. Sarah's heart sank, and the tears welled up again. "Great news," she said, sounding as dull as she felt.

"And you'll never guess who he is!"

"No, I imagine I won't."

"Sar-rah!"

That voice came from outside. Sarah froze. It was Alex. She wiped away her tears, then sniffed deeply. To heck with him. He wasn't here to plead with her to accept his love. He'd probably locked himself out, maybe left a briefcase inside. The briefcase could rot as far as she was concerned.

"Sarah! Sarah Nevins!"

It wasn't like Alex to be shouting her name to the neighborhood. Something must be terribly wrong. He'd hurt himself. He'd cracked up. "I have to go, Maude," she said, starting for the balcony.

"No, wait. I have to tell you…"

"Sarah Nevins!"

She reached the balcony and looked down.

"I love you," Alex shouted from below. "Will you marry me?"

"Omigosh," Sarah muttered. He was climbing the wisteria vine like a monkey, clinging to it with one hand.

"Later," Sarah said to the sound of Maude's voice going endlessly on. She ended the call and shoved the phone in her pocket.

"Alex," she hissed, "what the hell are you doing?"

"I'm coming back to get you, Sarah! A little thing like a locked door won't keep me away!"

"Get off that vine, Alex. You'll kill yourself."

"Who cares?" He swung one foot up to a notch in the vine and with one hand pulled himself up a few more feet.

He'd gone insane. It happened to people sometimes. She'd just never imagined, couldn't imagine in a million years, that it would ever happen to Alex. When someone went insane, you were supposed to be calm and soothing.

"Okay, Alex, let's act like grown-ups here. You get off the vine and go around to the front door. I'll let you in. We'll talk some more."

"We already tried that and it didn't work. I'm going to try this." And he hoisted himself another foot or two.

Sarah became aware of their audience. The lunch party next door had scattered. Two of the men were apparently standing on chairs looking over the brick wall that separated the two properties. They were looking extremely upset.

"This is an outrage," she heard from one of the women. "Hadley, do something."

"What do you think you're doing, sir?" one man called out to Alex. "If there's any more disturbance I'll have to call the police."

"Hi," Alex called out. "I'm Alex Emerson. I'm going to be your new neighbor." He gestured toward Sarah.

She gasped when he almost lost his balance on the wisteria. "This is Sarah Nevins. If I have my way about it, she's going to be your new neighbor, too."

"I am not," Sarah yelled. "I never saw this man before in my life."

"She's lying," Alex said. "I'm in love with her and I'm going to marry her." With a loud *oof*, he made another lurch upward.

Now he was close enough that she didn't have to yell. "Alex, you're making a scene. Please, please—I know, a compromise." She spoke briskly. "Get off at the first balcony. I'll come down and let you in."

"When I start something, I finish it," Alex declared. "What I started was a proposal. If you'd accept it, then I might consider—" he paused for a mighty heave upward "—getting off this vine. But until then—"

"Alex, this is no way to make a decision." She was pleading with him now. Out of the corner of her eye she saw the white-haired man who seemed to be Hadley talking on the smallest cell phone she'd ever seen. There wasn't much doubt who he was talking to.

The sounds of sirens confirmed it, sirens that died down directly behind her. Next came the sounds of pounding feet, and then the dreaded shout, "Hold it right there, buddy!"

"Hello, Officers," Alex said. "My name is Alex Emerson, and I am in love with Sarah Nevins. Did you hear me?" He shouted the words. "I...love...Sarah...Nevins, and I want the world to know it!"

It was at that moment that Sarah realized what Alex was trying to prove. She stared at the nightmarish scene below her and felt all the anger drain out of her heart, leaving room for the love that filled it, love for Alex that she could finally give freely and openly. He was showing her that he would do anything for her, even, God forbid, make a scene.

"Oh, Alex," she murmured. But she had something more important to do than accept his offer of marriage. First she had to save Alex from his second trip to jail in the space of a single summer.

She hoped he didn't intend to make a habit of it.

THE POLICE HAD GONE. The lunch party next door had resumed, although Sarah saw an occasional wary eye turn in their direction. With their arms around each other, Sarah and Alex rocked together, Alex nuzzling kisses into her hair, she into his throat, between their words of regret and love. It felt so wonderful to be with Alex again she was actually buzzing.

Alex cleared his throat. "Is that your phone or mine?"

"Oh. I thought it was love," Sarah said, and pulled her cell phone from her pocket.

"We got worried about you." It was Macon's voice. "Maude called. Said you hung up on her."

Sarah smiled at Alex. "Did she tell you who the Village Voyeur turned out to be?" she asked Macon. Alex's eyes smiled back at her.

"One of her fans," Macon said, "studying every location she mentioned in her last book." He sounded impatient. "But Sarah, how…"

"No kidding!" Sarah laughed aloud. "Now I bet she's going to court to testify on his behalf."

"She did mention something of the sort. But I want to know if you're all right."

"I'm fine," she said softly as Alex moved up to put his arm around her and bury his mouth in her neck. "Everything's fine."

Macon hesitated, as if he still didn't quite believe her.

"Should we start planning the move then? Because we can save a chunk of money on the van if we reserve it now."

She frowned. "What van?"

"The van we're taking to California."

"Macon—"

"Some of us around here are a little pinched financially, so we decided we'd—"

"Macon!"

"Oh, by the way. Bart wants to go along. Any problem with that? Everybody here's okay with it as long as Jeremy can still take his cactus."

"His *cactus?* Oh, Macon, you've got it all wrong. Listen. Don't do anything. I mean that literally. All of you go home, take the weekend off. What happened is—"

She caught sight of Alex's right hand for the first time. It was twice the size of his left hand.

"I've got to make a little trip to the emergency room," she said in a rush. "I'll tell you all about it on Monday."

"I'm not going to the—" Alex started to say.

"Sarah! What did that guy do to—" Macon yelled.

It was time to hang up on Macon and be extremely forceful with Alex. "We certainly are," she told him, circling him with her arm and nudging him toward the stairs. "On the way, I want to talk to you about going straight. I can't handle not knowing when I might look out the window and find you in handcuffs."

Alex decided to get one thing straight once and for all. He dug in his heels. "Would you go for stuffy?" He gave her a narrow-eyed gaze.

"Stuffy?" she said. "I don't know. Why would you want to be stuffy?"

"You always said I was."

"I never said you were stuffy. The very idea!"

Maybe she hadn't. Maybe he'd just sensed her thinking it. "Oh, all right," he said, "I'll give up on my dream of being stuffy."

"Prove it," she said.

"Happy to," he said, and kissed her.

LIVE THE EMOTION

Modern Romance™
...seduction and
passion guaranteed

Tender Romance™
...love affairs that
last a lifetime

Medical Romance™
...medical drama
on the pulse

Historical Romance™
...rich, vivid and
passionate

Sensual Romance™
...sassy, sexy and
seductive

Blaze Romance™
...the temperature's
rising

27 new titles every month.

Live the emotion

MILLS & BOON®

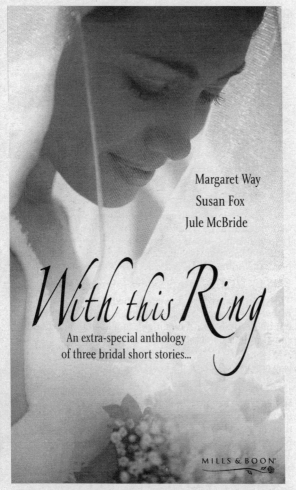

Margaret Way

Susan Fox

Jule McBride

With this Ring

An extra-special anthology
of three bridal short stories...

MILLS & BOON

Available from 18th April 2003

*Available at most branches of WH Smith,
Tesco, Martins, Borders, Eason, Sainsbury's
and all good paperback bookshops.*

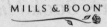